# MURDER
## IN E MINOR

*· A NERO WOLFE MYSTERY ·*

# MURDER
# IN E MINOR

## Robert Goldsborough

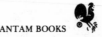

BANTAM BOOKS

TORONTO · NEW YORK · LONDON · SYDNEY · AUCKLAND

The author wishes to thank the estate of
the late Rex Stout for its cooperation and
encouragement.

MURDER IN E MINOR
*A Bantam Book / April 1986*

Library of Congress Cataloging-in-Publication Data
Goldsborough, Robert.
    Murder in E minor.

    I. Title.
PS3557.03849M8      1986      813.54      85–48045
ISBN 0-553-05123-7

*Published simultaneously in the United States and Canada*

*Bantam Books are published by Bantam Books, Inc. Its trademark, consisting of the*
*words "Bantam Books" and the portrayal of a rooster, is Registered in U.S. Patent*
*and Trademark Office and in other countries. Marca Registrada. Bantam Books,*
*Inc., 666 Fifth Avenue, New York, New York 10103.*

PRINTED IN THE UNITED STATES OF AMERICA

BP      0  9  8  7  6  5  4  3  2  1

*In memory of my mother,
who first introduced me to Nero Wolfe
and Archie Goodwin.*

# FOREWORD

I realize that a lot was written and broadcast about the case that follows, not just in New York, but across the country. However, nobody, not even Lon Cohen's *Gazette*, had the space or the knowledge to come anywhere close to giving the whole account. I didn't think it would ever get printed anywhere, for that matter. Let me explain. Because this episode was such a personal one for Nero Wolfe, he didn't feel I ought to write about it. And because he signs my weekly checks, I went along with him, at least for a while. Even Wolfe can be worn down by badgering, though. It took me a long time (I didn't bring the subject up all that often), but he finally gave in, years after the fact. He didn't give me any reasons, he just nodded, probably to shut me up. Now you know.

ARCHIE GOODWIN

# 1

Nero Wolfe and I have argued for years about whether the client who makes his first visit to us before or after noon is more likely to provide an interesting—and lucrative—case. Wolfe contends that the average person is incapable of making a rational decision, such as hiring him, until he or she has had a minimum of two substantial meals that day. My own feeling is that the caller with the greater potential is the one who has spent the night agonizing, finally realizes at dawn that Wolfe is the answer, and does something about it fast. I'll leave it to you to decide, based on our past experience, which of us has it better pegged.

I'd have been more smug about the timing of Maria Radovich's call that rainy morning if I'd thought there was even one chance in twenty that Wolfe would see her, let alone go back to work. It had been more than two years since Orrie Cather committed suicide—with Wolfe's blessing and mine. At the time, the realization that one of his longtime standbys had murdered three people didn't seem to bother Wolfe, but since then I had come to see that the whole business had rocked him pretty good. He would never admit it, of course, with that ego fit for his seventh of a ton, but he was still stung that someone who for years had sat at his table, drunk his liquor, and followed his orders could be a cool and deliberate killer. And even though the D.A. had reinstated both our licenses shortly after Orrie's death, Wolfe had stuck his head in the sand and still hadn't pulled it out. I tried needling him back to work, a tactic that had been successful in the past, but I got stonewalled, to use a word he hates.

"Archie," he would say, looking up from his book, "as I have told you many times, one of your most commendable attributes through the years has been your ability to badger me into working. That former asset is now a liability. You may goad me if you wish, but it is futile. I will not take the bait. And desist using the word 'retired.' I prefer to say that I have withdrawn from practice." And with that, he would return to his book, which currently was a rereading of *Emma* by Jane Austen.

It wasn't that we did not have opportunities. One well-fixed Larchmont widow offered twenty grand for starters if Wolfe would find out who poisoned her chauffeur, and I couldn't even get him to see her. The murder was never solved, although I leaned toward the live-in maid, who was losing out in a triangle to the gardener's daughter. Then there was the Wall Street money man—you'd know his name right off—who said Wolfe could set his own price if only we'd investigate his son's death. The police and the coroner had called it a suicide, but the father was convinced it was a narcotics-related murder. Wolfe politely but firmly turned the man down in a ten-minute conversation in the office, and the kid's death went on the books as a suicide.

I couldn't even use the money angle to stir him. On

a few of our last big cases, Wolfe insisted on having the payments spread over a long period, so that a series of checks—some of them biggies—rolled in every month. That, coupled with a bunch of good investments, gave him a cash flow that was easily sufficient to operate the old brownstone on West Thirty-fifth Street near the Hudson that has been home to me for more than half my life. And operating the brownstone doesn't come cheap, because Nero Wolfe has costly tastes. They include my salary as his confidential assistant, errand boy, and—until two years ago—man of action, as well as those of Theodore Horstmann, nurse to the ten thousand orchids Wolfe grows in the plant rooms up on the roof, and Fritz Brenner, on whom I would bet in a cook-off against any other chef in the universe.

I still had the standard chores, such as maintaining the orchid germination records, paying the bills, figuring the taxes, and handling Wolfe's correspondence. But I had lots of free time now, and Wolfe didn't object to a little free-lancing. I did occasional work for Del Bascomb, a first-rate local operative, and also teamed with Saul Panzer on a couple of jobs, including the Masters kidnapping case, which you may have read about. Wolfe went so far as to compliment me on that one, so at least I knew he still read about crime, although he refused to let me talk about it in his presence anymore.

Other than having put his brain in the deep freeze, Wolfe kept his routine pretty much the same as ever: breakfast on a tray in his room; four hours a day—9 to 11 A.M. and 4 to 6 P.M.—in the plant rooms with Theodore; long conferences with Fritz on menus and food preparation; and the best meals in Manhattan. The rest of the time, he was in his oversized chair behind his desk in the office reading and drinking beer. And refusing to work.

Maria Radovich's call came at nine-ten on Tuesday morning, which meant Wolfe was up with the plants. Fritz was in the kitchen working on one of Wolfe's favorite lunches, sweetbreads in bechamel sauce and truffles. I answered at my desk, where I was balancing the checkbook.

"Nero Wolfe's residence. Archie Goodwin speaking."

"I need to see Mr. Wolfe—today. May I make an appointment?" It was the voice of a young woman, shaky, and with an accent that seemed familiar to me.

"I'm sorry, but Mr. Wolfe isn't consulting at the present time," I said, repeating a line I had grown to hate.

"Please, it's important that I see him. I think my—"

"Look, Mr. Wolfe isn't seeing anyone, honest. I can suggest some agencies if you're looking for a private investigator."

"No, I want Mr. Nero Wolfe. My uncle has spoken of him, and I am sure he would want to help. My uncle knew Mr. Wolfe many years ago in Montenegro, and—"

"Where?" I barked it out.

"In Montenegro. They grew up there together. And now I am frightened about my uncle . . ."

Ever since it became widely known that Wolfe had retired—make that "withdrawn from practice"—would-be clients had cooked up some dandy stories to try to get him working again. I was on their side, but I knew Wolfe well enough to realize that almost nothing would bring him back to life. This was the first time, though, that anyone had been ingenious enough to come up with a Montenegro angle, and I admire ingenuity.

"I'm sorry to hear that you're scared," I said, "but Mr. Wolfe is pretty hard-hearted. I've got a reputation as a softie, though. How soon can your uncle be here? I'm Mr. Wolfe's confidential assistant, and I'll be glad to see him, Miss . . ."

"Radovich, Maria Radovich. Yes, I recognized your

name. My uncle doesn't know I am calling. He would be angry. But I will come right away, if it's all right."

I assured her it was indeed all right and hung up, staring at the open checkbook. It was a long shot, no question, but if I had anything to lose by talking to her, I couldn't see it. And just maybe, the Montenegro bit was for real. Montenegro, in case you don't know, is a small piece of Yugoslavia, and it's where Wolfe comes from. He still has relatives there; I send checks to three of them every month. But as for old friends, I doubted any were still alive. His closest friend ever, Marko Vukcic, had been murdered years ago, and the upshot was that Wolfe and I went tramping off to the Montenegrin mountains to avenge his death. And although Wolfe was anything but gabby about his past, I figured I knew just about enough to eliminate the possibility of a close comrade popping up. But there's no law against hoping.

I got a good, leisurely look at her through the one-way glass in the front door as she stood in the drizzle ringing our bell. Dark-haired, dark-eyed, and slender, she had a touch of Mia Farrow in her face. And like Farrow in several of her roles, she seemed frightened and unsure. But looking through the glass, I was convinced that with Maria Radovich, it was no act.

She jumped when I opened the door. "Oh! Mr. Goodwin?"

"The selfsame," I answered with a slight bow and an earnest smile. "And you are Maria Radovich, I presume? Please come in out of the twenty-percent chance of showers."

I hung her trench coat on the hall rack and motioned toward the office. Walking behind her, I could see that her figure, set off by a skirt of fashionable length, was a bit fuller than I remembered Mia Farrow's to be, and that was okay with me.

"Mr. Wolfe doesn't come down to the office for another hour and ten minutes," I said, motioning to the yellow chair nearest my desk. "Which is fine, because he wouldn't see you anyway. At least not right now. He thinks he's retired from the detective business. But I'm not." I flipped open my notebook and swiveled to face her.

"I'm sure if Mr. Wolfe knew about my uncle's trouble, he would want to do something right away," she said, twisting a scarf in her lap and leaning forward tensely.

"You don't know him, Miss Radovich. He can be immovable, irascible, and exasperating when he wants to, which is most of the time. I'm afraid you're stuck with me, at least for now. Maybe we can get Mr. Wolfe interested later, but to do that, I've got to know everything. Like for starters, who is your uncle and why are you worried about him?"

"He is my great-uncle, really," she answered, still using only the front quarter of the chair cushion. "And he is very well-known. Milan Stevens. I am sure you have heard of him—he is music director, some people say conductor, of the New York Symphony."

Not wanting to look stupid or disappoint her, or both, I nodded. I've been to the Symphony four or five times, always with Lily Rowan, and it was always her idea. Milan Stevens may have been the conductor one or more of those times, but I wouldn't take an oath on it. The name was only vaguely familiar.

"Mr. Goodwin, for the last two weeks my uncle has been getting letters in the mail—awful, vile letters. I think someone may want to kill him, but he just throws the letters away. I am frightened. I am sure that—"

"How many letters have there been, Miss Radovich? Do you have any of them?"

She nodded and reached into the shoulder bag she had set on the floor. "Three so far, all the same." She handed the crumpled sheets over, along with their envelopes, and I spread them on my desk. Each was on six-by-nine-inch notepaper, plain white, the kind from an inexpensive tear-off pad. They were hand-printed, in all caps, with a black felt-tip pen. One read:

MAESTRO
QUIT THE PODIUM NOW! YOU ARE
DOING DAMAGE TO A GREAT ORCHESTRA
PUT DOWN THE BATON AND GET OUT
IF YOU DON'T LEAVE ON YOUR OWN,
YOU WILL BE REMOVED—PERMANENTLY!

In fact, all three weren't exactly alike. The wording differed, though only slightly. The "on your own" in the last sentence was missing from one note, and the first sentence didn't have an exclamation point in another. Maria had lightly penciled the numbers one, two, and three on the back of each to indicate the order in which they were received. The envelopes were of a similar ordinary stock, each hand-printed to Milan Stevens at an address in the East Seventies. "His apartment?" I asked.

Maria nodded. "Yes, he and I have lived there since we came to this country, a little over two years ago."

"Miss Radovich, before we talk more about these notes, tell me about your uncle, and yourself. First, you said on the phone that he and Mr. Wolfe knew each other in Montenegro."

She eased back into the chair and nodded. "Yes, my uncle—his real name is Stefanovic, Milos Stefanovic. We are from Yugoslavia. I was born in Belgrade, but my uncle is a Montenegrin. That's a place on the Adriatic. But of course I don't have to tell you that—I'm sure you know all about it from Mr. Wolfe.

"My uncle's been a musician and conductor all over Europe—Italy, Austria, Germany. He was conducting in London last, before we came here. But long ago, he did some fighting in Montenegro. I know little of it, but I think he was involved in an independence movement. He doesn't like to talk about that at all, and he never mentioned Mr. Wolfe to me until one time when his picture was in the papers. It was something to do with a murder or a suicide—I think maybe your picture was there too?"

I nodded. That would have been when Orrie died. "What did your uncle say about Mr. Wolfe?"

"I gather they had lost touch over the years. But he didn't seem at all interested in trying to reach Mr. Wolfe. At the time I said, 'How wonderful that such an old friend is right here. What a surprise! You'll call him, of course?' But Uncle Milos said no, that was part of the past. And I got the idea from the way he acted that they must have had some kind of difference. But that was so long ago!"

"If you sensed your uncle was unfriendly toward Mr. Wolfe, what made you call?"

"After he told me about knowing Mr. Wolfe back in Montenegro, Uncle Milos kept looking at the picture in the paper and nodding his head. He said to me, 'He had the finest mind I have ever known. I wish I could say the same for his disposition.' "

I held back a smile. "But you got the impression that your uncle and Mr. Wolfe were close at one time?"

"Absolutely," Maria said. "Uncle Milos told me they had been through some great difficulty together. He even showed me this picture from an old scrapbook." She reached again into her bag and handed me a gray-toned photograph mounted on cardboard and ragged around the edges.

They certainly fit my conception of a band of guerrillas, although none looked to be out of his teens. There were nine in all, posed in front of a high stone wall, four kneeling in front and five standing behind them.

Some were wearing long overcoats, others had on woolen shirts, and two wore what I think of as World War I helmets. I spotted Wolfe instantly, of course. He was second from the left in the back row, with his hands behind his back and a bandolier slung over one shoulder. His hair was darker then, and he weighed at least one hundred pounds less, but the face was remarkably similar to the one I had looked at across the dinner table last night. And his glare had the same intensity, coming at me from a faded picture, that it does in the office when he thinks I'm badgering him.

To Wolfe's right in the photo was Marko Vukcic, holding a rifle loosely at his side. "Which one's your uncle?" I asked Maria.

She leaned close enough so I could smell her perfume and pointed to one of the kneelers in front. He was dark-haired and intense like most of the others, but he appeared smaller than most of them. None of the nine, though, looked as if he were trying to win a congeniality contest. If they were as tough as they appeared, I'm glad I wasn't fighting against them.

"This picture was taken up in the mountains," Maria said. "Uncle Milos only showed it to me to point out Mr. Wolfe, but he wouldn't talk any more about the other men or what they were doing."

"Not going to a picnic," I said. "I'd like to hang onto this for a while. Now, what about you, Miss Radovich? How does it happen you're living with a great-uncle?"

She told me about how her mother, a widow, had died when she was a child in Yugoslavia, and that Stefanovic, her mother's uncle, had legally adopted her. Divorced and without children, he was happy to have the companionship of a nine-year-old. Maria said he gave her all the love of a parent, albeit a strict one, taking her with him as he moved around Europe to increasingly better and more prestigious conducting jobs. At some time before moving to England, he had changed his name to Stevens—she couldn't remember exactly when. It was while they were living in London that he was picked as the new conductor, or music director if you prefer, of the New York Symphony. Maria, who by that time was twenty-three, made the move with him, and she was now a dancer with a small troupe in New York.

"Mr. Goodwin," she said, leaning forward and tensing again, "my uncle has worked hard all his life to get the kind of position and recognition he has today. Now somebody is trying to take it away from him." Her hand gripped my forearm.

"Why not just go to the police?" I asked with a shrug.

"I suggested that to Uncle Milos, and he became very angry. He said it would leak out to the newspapers and cause a scandal at the Symphony, that the publicity would be harmful to him and the orchestra. He says these notes are from a crazy person, or maybe someone playing a prank. I was with him when he opened the first one, or I might not know about any of this. He read it and said something that means 'stupid' in Serbo-Croatian, then crumpled the note and threw it in the wastebasket. But he hardly spoke the rest of the evening.

"I waited until he left the room to get the note from the basket. It was then that I said we should call the police. He became upset and said it was probably a prankster, or maybe a season-ticket holder who didn't like the music the orchestra had been playing."

"How long until the next note?" I asked.

"I started watching the mail after that. Six days later, we got another envelope printed just like the first one. I didn't open it—I never open my uncle's mail. But again I found the crumpled note in the wastebasket next to his desk in the library. This time I didn't mention it to him, and he said nothing about it to me, but again he seemed distressed.

"The third note came yesterday, six days after the second, and again I found it in the wastebasket. Uncle Milos doesn't know that I've seen the last two notes, or that I've saved all three."

"Miss Radovich, does your uncle have any enemies you know of, anyone who would gain by his leaving the Symphony?"

"The music director of a large orchestra always has his detractors." She took a deep breath. "There are always people who think it can be done better. Some are jealous, others just take pleasure in scoffing at talented people. My uncle does not discuss his work very much at home, but I do know, from him and from others, that he has opposition even within the orchestra. But notes like this, I can't believe—"

"*Someone* is writing them, Miss Radovich. I'd like to hear more about your uncle's opposition, but Mr. Wolfe will be down in just a few minutes, and it's best if you're not here when he comes in. He may get interested in your problem, but you'll have to let me be the one to try getting him interested."

For the third time, Maria dove into her bag. She fished out a wad of bills and thrust it at me. "There's five hundred dollars here," she said. "That is just for agreeing to try to find out who's writing the notes. I can pay another forty-five hundred dollars if you discover the person and get him to stop." Five grand was a long way below what Wolfe usually got as a fee, but I figured that for Maria Radovich, it was probably big bucks. I started to return the money, then I drew back and smiled.

"Fair enough," I said. "If I can get Nero Wolfe to move, we keep this. Otherwise, it goes back to you. Now we've got to get you out of here. You'll be hearing from me soon—one way or the other." I wrote her a receipt for the money, keeping a carbon, and hustled her out to the hall and on with her coat.

My watch said ten fifty-eight as she went down the steps to the street. I rushed back to the office, put the money and receipt in the safe, and arranged Wolfe's morning mail in a pile on his blotter. Included in the stack was one item the carrier hadn't delivered: a faded fifty-year-old photograph.

## 2

I just had time to get my paper in the typewriter and start on yesterday's dictation when I heard
the elevator coming down from the plant rooms. "Good
morning, Archie, did you sleep well?" he asked as he
walked across to his desk, arranged a raceme of purple
Cattleyas in the vase, then settled his bulk into the only
chair he likes and rang for beer.

"Yes, sir," I answered, looking up. Despite his size,
and we're talking about a seventh of a ton here, I've
never gotten used to how efficient Wolfe is when he
moves. Somehow, you keep thinking he's going to trip
or do something clumsy when he goes around behind
his desk, but he never does. Everything is smooth, even
graceful—if you can use that word with someone so
large. Then there are his clothes. Fat people get a rap
for being sloppy, but not Nero Wolfe. Today, as usual,
he was wearing a three-piece suit, this one a tan tweed,
with a fresh yellow shirt and a brown silk tie with
narrow yellow stripes. His wavy hair, still brown but

with a healthy dose of gray mixed in, was carefully brushed. He'd never admit it to me or anybody else, but Nero Wolfe spent his share of time in front of the mirror every morning, and that included shaving with a straight razor, something I quit trying years ago when I got tired of the sight of my own blood.

I kept sneaking glances at Wolfe while he riffled through the stack of mail. The photograph was about halfway down, but he took his time getting there, stopping as I knew he would to peruse a seed catalog. I typed on.

"Archie!" It was a high-grade bellow, the first one he'd uncorked in months.

I looked up, feigning surprise.

"Where did this come from?" he asked, jabbing at the picture.

"What's that, sir?" I raised one eyebrow, which always gets him because he can't do it.

"You know very well. How did this get here? What envelope was it in?"

"Oh, *that*. Well, let me think . . . yes, of course, I almost forgot. It was brought by a young woman, nice-looking, too. She thought you might be interested in helping her with a problem."

Wolfe glowered, then leaned forward and studied the photograph. "They must all be dead by now. . . . Two were killed by firing squads, one died in a foolhardy duel, another drowned in the Adriatic. And Marko . . ."

"They're not *all* dead," I put in. "You aren't, not legally anyway, although you've been putting on a good imitation for a couple of years. And there's at least one other living man in that picture."

Wolfe went back to the photograph, this time for more than a minute. "*Stefanovic*." He pronounced it far differently than I would have. "I have no knowledge of his death."

"You win a case of salt-water taffy," I said. "Not only

is he still breathing, but he lives right here in New York. And what's more, he's famous. Of course he's changed his name since you knew him."

Wolfe shot me another glower. His index finger was tracing circles on the arm of the chair, the only outward indication that he was furious. I knew more than he did about something and was forcing him to ask questions, which made it even worse.

"Archie, I have suffered your contumacy for longer than I care to think about." He pursed his lips. "Confound it, report!"

"Yes, sir," I said, maintaining a somber expression. Then I unloaded everything verbatim, from Maria's phone call to the money. When I got to the part about the three notes, I opened the safe and pulled them out, but he refused to give them a glance. During my whole report, he sat with his eyes closed, fingers interlaced on his center mound. He interrupted twice to ask questions. When I was through, he sat in silence, eyes still closed.

After about five minutes, I said, "Are you asleep, or just waiting for me to call in a portrait painter so he can capture your favorite pose?"

"Archie, shut up!" That made it two bellows in one day. I was trying to think up something smart to say that would bring on a third and set a record, but Fritz came in and announced lunch.

Wolfe has a rule, never broken, that business is not to be discussed during meals, and it had been an easy rule to keep for the last two years, since there wasn't any business. That day, though, my mind was on other things and I barely tasted Fritz's superb sweetbreads. Wolfe, however, consumed three helpings at his normal, unhurried pace, while holding forth on the reasons why third parties have been unsuccessful in American elections.

We finally went back to the office for coffee. During

lunch, I decided I'd pushed Wolfe enough and would leave the next move to him. We sat in silence for several minutes, and I was beginning to revise my strategy when he got up and went to the bookshelf. He pulled down the big atlas, lugged it back to his desk, and opened it. He looked at a page, then turned back to the photograph, fingering it gently.

"Archie?" He drew in a bushel of air, then let it out slowly.

"Yes, sir?"

"You know Montenegro, at least superficially."

"Yes, sir."

"You also know—I have told you—that in my youth there, I was impetuous and headstrong, and that I sometimes showed a pronounced lack of judgment."

"So you have said."

"A half-century ago in Montenegro, Milos Stefanovic and I were relatively close friends, although I never shared his consuming interest in music. We fought together, along with Marko and others in the photograph, for a cause in which we strongly believed. On one occasion in Cetinje, Stefanovic saved my life. And then, for reasons that are now irrelevant, he and I parted, not without rancor. I haven't seen him since that time, and I probably haven't thought about him for twenty years, at least. I mention this by way of telling you that we are faced with an extraordinary circumstance."

"Yes, sir." Although Wolfe's upstairs horsepower is far greater than mine, I've been around long enough to know when he's rationalizing. I stifled a smile.

"I am duty-bound to see this woman." He spread his hands in what for him is a dramatic gesture of helplessness. "I have no choice. Tell her to be here at three o'clock. Also, it's been a long time since Mr. Cohen has joined us for dinner. Call and invite him for tonight.

And tell him we will be serving that cognac he enjoys so much."

I was delighted, of course, that Wolfe had agreed to see Maria. But his wanting Lon Cohen to come for dinner was a bonus. Lon works for the *Gazette,* where he has an office two doors from the publisher's on the twentieth floor. He doesn't have a title I'm aware of, but I can't remember a major story in New York that he didn't know more about than ever appeared in the *Gazette,* or anyplace else, for that matter. Lon and I play in the same weekly poker game, but he only comes to dinner at Wolfe's a couple of times a year, and it's almost always when Wolfe wants information. This is all right with Lon, because he's gotten a fat file of exclusive stories from us through the years, not to mention some three-star meals.

As it turned out, Lon was available, although he wanted to know what was up. I told him he'd just have to wait, and that there was some Remisier to warm his tummy after dinner. He said for that he'd sell any state secrets he had lying around his office. And Maria could make it at three. "Does this mean Mr. Wolfe will take the case?" she asked over the phone breathlessly.

"Who knows?" I answered. "But at least he'll see you, and that alone is progress."

I went to the kitchen to tell Fritz there would be a guest for dinner. "Archie, things are happening today, I can tell. Is he going back to work?"

Fritz always fusses when Wolfe is in one of his periodic relapses. He acts like we're on the brink of bankruptcy at all times and thinks that if Wolfe isn't constantly performing feats of detection, there won't be enough money to pay his salary or, more important, the food bills. Needless to say, the last two years of inactivity by Wolfe had left Fritz with a permanently long puss, and I more than once caught him in the kitchen wringing his hands, looking heavenward, and muttering things in French. "Archie, he needs to work," Fritz would say. "He enjoys his food more then. Work sharpens his appetite." I always replied that his appetite seemed plenty sharp to me, but he just shook his head mournfully.

This time, though, I was delighted to report that prospects were improving. "Keep your carving knives crossed," I told him, "and say a prayer to Brillat-Savarin."

"I'll do more than that," he said. "Tonight, you and Mr. Wolfe and Mr. Cohen will have a dinner to remember." Whistling, he turned to his work, and I whistled a bit myself on the way back to the office.

## 3

Maria was ten minutes early, and she looked as frightened as she had that morning. She'd changed and was wearing a soft Angora peaches-and-cream-colored number, one of those dresses that seems equally appropriate for daytime wear or for dinner and dancing. I wanted to put my arms around her, but I sat her in the red leather chair instead, and once again arranged the three notes to Stefanovic on Wolfe's desk blotter. Even geniuses need reference material.

Wolfe was in the kitchen with Fritz conferring on dinner: beef tournedos with sauce béarnaise, squash with sour cream and dill, celery-and-cantaloupe salad, and blueberry tart. When I told him Maria had arrived, he grimaced. The idea of having a woman in the house revolts him, and it's all the worse if her presence means he'll have to go to work. I went back to the office, and two minutes later he walked in, detoured around Maria, and dipped his head an eighth of an inch before sitting. That's his version of a bow.

"Madam," he said, "Mr. Goodwin has informed me of your earlier visit. He also told you, correctly, that I am no longer actively practicing as a private investigator. But your uncle—if indeed he is that—is an individual to whom I owe an incalculable debt. That debt alone is sufficient reason for my seeing you.

"Let me forewarn you, however," he said, waggling a finger at her, "that this discussion is not tantamount to a contract."

Maria nodded slowly, but she was frowning. "Mr. Wolfe, you said 'if indeed he is that.' Do you question that I am the niece of—"

Wolfe cut her off, but I can't report what he said because it was in Serbo-Croatian, of which I know maybe fifteen words. He spoke what sounded like two or three sentences, and Maria responded in the same tongue. They went back and forth for about a minute. Then Wolfe nodded and turned to me. "Archie, I asked Miss Radovich several questions that only someone close to Milos Stefanovic could have answered. I am satisfied with her replies. If you want the substance of our conversation, I'll supply it later."

"No problem," I said. "I've been secretly studying Serbo-Croatian on records up in my room for the last eight years, and I've taken down everything you said in shorthand."

Wolfe glared at me and turned back to Maria. "I understand from Mr. Goodwin that your uncle is unaware of your visit. Also, he apparently wants to avoid any revelation of these notes?"

Maria nodded. "Uncle Milos became extremely upset when I suggested he go to the police."

Wolfe's eyes narrowed. "Miss Radovich, who sent these to your uncle?"

"Well, I . . . if I knew, I wouldn't have come to you. That's what I was hoping you would find out."

"Come now," Wolfe said, leaning forward. "Surely you don't take Mr. Goodwin and me for lackwits. You must have some suspicion—a strong one—about who is harassing your uncle. And you want us to either confirm or reject that suspicion. That is why you're here."

"I am here because I want to know who sent those notes, and I want to know how serious the threats in them are to my uncle," Maria answered evenly, returning Wolfe's gaze without blinking. Her fright seemed to have evaporated, although her hands were still clenched tightly in her lap.

Wolfe's shoulders rose and fell a fraction of an inch. "Very well. You told Mr. Goodwin that your uncle had enemies within the orchestra. Let us proceed in that direction."

"I also told Mr. Goodwin that it is not unusual for the conductor of a major orchestra to find strong opposition. Name a famous conductor, and almost surely he has encountered difficulties."

"But *mortal* difficulties?" Wolfe said, raising his eyebrows. "I don't know enough, or care enough, about symphony orchestras to be able to name their conductors, but I can't recall ever hearing of threats on one's life, and mortal threats are implied in these notes. Madam, I cannot fire without powder. Surely you can suggest someone who would benefit from your uncle's departure from the orchestra." He turned a palm over. "A past grudge? A slight? Jealousy? Disagreement over artistic competence?"

"I just can't believe that anyone connected with the Symphony would—"

"You felt these notes warranted a visit to me. Now you have my attention. You seek aid; we can give none without your full cooperation. If you choose to deflect my questions, it is fruitless to continue."

Maria winced. "I'm sorry. Of course you're right." She paused, picking her way. "When my uncle was chosen to be the Symphony's music director, the decision was not popular with everyone. But Jason Remmers—the board chairman of the Symphony—insisted on hiring Uncle Milos. He had talked to him several times in London, and was very persuasive in getting him to move to this country."

"Remmers—of the beer family?" Wolfe asked.

"I'm not sure, but I think perhaps that is right," Maria said.

Wolfe nodded. Remmers is his brand, and has been almost as long as I've known him, which means he's probably consumed a freight-train full at his rate of intake. He used the opportunity to finish the first of two bottles Fritz had brought in. "Who opposed Mr. Remmers's choice?" he asked as he poured the other bottle into his glass.

"Mr. Meyerhoff, the orchestra's managing director, was against Uncle Milos from the start. He felt, or so I've heard, that my uncle is too strict, too demanding."

"And too difficult to get along with?" Wolfe purred.

"Yes, that too. You knew my uncle, Mr. Wolfe; he is a perfectionist. He will not accept anything less than the maximum efforts from his musicians. If he is demanding, it is because he wants the finest possible performance. Mr. Remmers was aware of that when he came to London. Uncle Milos had a reputation there as a firm leader, and the Symphony needed someone firm. But Mr. Meyerhoff and Mr. Hirsch were hostile to him from the start."

"Mr. Hirsch?" Wolfe asked.

"David Hirsch, the associate conductor of the orchestra," Maria said.

"Was Mr. Hirsch associate conductor when Milos Stefanovic joined the orchestra?" Wolfe asked.

"Yes, and that is part of the problem. He is said to have wanted the conductor's job for himself at the time. From the day my uncle arrived in New York, they have had what you would call strained relations, although Mr. Hirsch has always been very pleasant to me. And so has Mr. Meyerhoff, for that matter."

"Have any other members of the orchestra or staff feuded with your uncle?" Wolfe asked.

Maria paused for several seconds before shaking her head. "No . . . other than perhaps the usual resentment of musicians toward a strict conductor. At least none that I've heard of."

"Miss Radovich, does your uncle have close friends in New York? Persons he sees socially?"

Another pause. "Uncle Milos has never made friends easily. He likes to be alone. But there is one *woman* . . ." She came down hard on the last word.

"Yes?" Wolfe prodded.

Maria pursed her lips. "She and Uncle Milos go to the theater often, and to parties. She has him for dinner, and sometimes she comes to our apartment after concerts for a drink or late supper."

"Her name?"

"Lucinda Forrester-Moore. She's a widow, and well-known in society. Her picture is in the newspapers a lot."

No argument there. Lucinda Forrester-Moore's name seemed to pop up in at least one of the columns every few days, and she was a favorite subject for the photographers, too. The *Gazette* picture file on her was probably bulging. Lily Rowan had introduced us a couple of years back, I think at Rusterman's restaurant, and while she has a few too many years on her for my taste, I have to admit that for an older model, she still looks to be in good running condition. Uncle Milos was doing all right.

"Is your uncle's relationship with this woman a romantic one?" Wolfe asked.

"I wish I could say no," Maria answered. "But I think he is . . . very interested. And she is a *hunter*." She hit the arm of the chair with a fist. "She has always chased famous men—she is known for it. But Uncle Milos can't see that. I've tried to tell him—"

"Is this relationship approaching marriage, Miss Radovich?" Wolfe asked.

"Lord, I hope not!" I jumped at the intensity of her answer, and I think it scared Maria herself. She blushed becomingly and cleared her throat before going on. "Uncle Milos has said several times through the years that he has no interest in getting married again."

"Mr. Goodwin mentioned to me that your uncle had been married once years ago," Wolfe said. "Is his former wife alive?"

"Yes. She is a lovely and gracious woman, Mr. Wolfe. She and Uncle Milos were divorced before I was born, and she moved to London."

"Who is she?" Wolfe asked.

"Her name is Alexandra Adjari. I met her for the first time when Uncle Milos and I settled in London and he took the conducting job there. They were not on friendly terms, but she wanted to get to know me."

"She's back to her maiden name," Wolfe said. It wasn't a question.

"Yes, she never remarried. I think she had money of her own, from before she knew Uncle Milos. She has a large flat in Mayfair."

"Just so," said Wolfe. "Have you communicated with her recently?"

"We write at Christmas, but that's all, and I haven't seen her since Uncle Milos and I moved here from London," Maria said.

Wolfe started in on the orchestra again; I'd forgotten how good his technique was when he felt like working, and this was the closest he'd come to working in a long time. He chatted with Maria about orchestras in general, then gradually worked his way to individuals before retreating to generalities again. He repeated this over and over, and I filled at least two dozen notebook pages with the conversation, but these samples will give you the flavor of the entire session:

W: How many musicians does the orchestra have?

M: It varies depending on the particular piece being played, but for a big symphonic number, there are over a hundred onstage, I think.

W: Do they always occupy the same seats?

M: Basically, except for some shuffling around when special instruments are used.

W: Such as?

M: Oh, guitar, glockenspiel, celesta, things like that.

And on another page:

W: Are there women in the orchestra?

M: Oh, yes.

W: How many: Ten? Fifty?

M: I don't know—maybe about fifteen.

W: Has your uncle ever had a particular interest in any one of them?

M: (blushing) No, never. That would be grossly unprofessional, and Uncle Milos is very strict about things like that. He keeps his private life totally separate from his work.

W: How does he feel about liaisons between orchestra members?

M: (blushing again) I really don't know. It's never come up that I'm aware of.

And further on in my notes:

W: Do you know many members of the orchestra well?

M: (pausing) Just a few. I've met some at parties, receptions, things like that.

W: As a group, do you like musicians?

M: I . . . well, it's like anything else; it depends on the individual, some are nice people, some . . . aren't so nice.

W: Do you have an active dislike for anyone in the orchestra?

M: No, I really couldn't say that. No.

W: (leaning forward slightly) What about a particular fondness?

M: (slight pause) I'm pretty busy with my dancing and don't really spend much time around the orchestra or Symphony Hall. When we're not at home, Uncle Milos and I move in separate circles.

And so it went. In all, Wolfe kept at it for almost an hour, and each time he asked her about specific relationships, she tightened up. I could tell when he began to lose interest. The questions got sillier, including one about what kind of clothes women orchestra members wear. About the time I was totally exasperated with him, Wolfe shifted in his chair and said, "Miss Radovich, I have another engagement; Mr. Goodwin knows how to reach you, I believe?"

Maria looked puzzled, nodded, then got up and thanked both of us. Wolfe remained seated as I followed her to the front hall, helped her on with her coat, and assured her I would call her no later than tomorrow.

"But I don't understand; is Mr. Wolfe going to help or not?" she asked.

"I've known him for years, but I don't understand him either, Miss Radovich. It's hell living in the same house with someone who thinks he's an eccentric genius. All I can promise is that I'll call by tomorrow with some kind of news." I opened the door for her and watched her walk down our front steps for the second time that day. When I got back to the office, Wolfe was scowling.

"She's withholding something, of course," he said.

I nodded. "She was too slow in answering a few times."

"She's trying to protect someone," he said. "Someone

she thinks might have written those notes. But she doesn't want to believe it."

"No argument here," I said.

"Your impression?" Wolfe asked. Over the years, he has convinced himself that I'm an expert on women, and I've tried my best to maintain the image. "Seems responsible and levelheaded, despite the nervousness," I said. "And certainly attractive. She probably has a man. I thought you would get into that a little more with her, but maybe you've lost your touch. Could be she's having an affair with someone in the orchestra, which raises all sorts of interesting possibilities."

Wolfe winced. "Talk to her. Take her dancing. Find out whom she's shielding." Having shown he was still capable of giving a direct order, he lifted his bulk out of the chair and headed for the elevator and his afternoon appointment with the orchids.

## 4

The three of us sat in the office with coffee and brandy, Wolfe and I at our desks and Lon in the red leather chair. Fritz had made good on his promise of a meal to remember: the beef tournedos had never been so good, and the blueberry tart got passed around the table twice. Dinner conversation had ranged from the role of the Palestinians in the Middle East to the future of American cities and the effectiveness of wage-price controls.

Lon passed a hand over his dark slicked-back hair and smiled. "As usual, I've had a splendid evening here, and if anything, the brandy has improved since the last time I had the honor of sampling it. But I know you well enough to realize this isn't strictly social. And tonight, I'm even more curious than in the past, because of your recent . . . inactivity."

"Mr. Cohen, we've been able to help each other on numerous occasions," Wolfe said between sips of coffee. "I'll repeat a question I've asked before: On balance, are we substantially even?"

Lon threw up a hand and laughed. "No complaints. None. As I've said in the past, I'm running ahead on the deal. If I've got an answer that can help in any way, it's yours."

Wolfe nodded. "For reasons I can't divulge now—and which indeed I may never be able to reveal—I need information on the operations and personnel of the New York Symphony Orchestra. Based on my experience with the scope of your knowledge on a variety of subjects, I'm confident you can supply this information."

Lon grinned and took another sip of Remisier. He was being flattered, none too subtly, by the best, and fattest, detective in New York and probably the world, and he didn't mind it a bit.

"I didn't realize you had an interest in orchestral music," he said, scratching his chin. "Well, I guess I know a fair amount about what goes on over at Symphony Hall. And if I don't, we've got a music critic with more pipelines than OPEC. Shoot."

Wolfe rang for beer and readjusted himself. "From what little I've learned about the orchestra, it appears that some tensions exist among its principals, both the performers and the management. Do you know this to be the case?"

"That's a delicate way of putting it," Lon said. "The truth is that the Symphony's been a jungle for several years. There was a string of weak music directors, none of them able to control the orchestra. Then they brought this guy Stevens over from England a couple years ago, and he has a reputation as one tough cookie. But if anything, the situation seems to have gotten worse."

"Is all the bickering a manifestation of artistic temperaments?" Wolfe asked. He had never thought much of highbrow music or the people who made it.

"That's part of it of course," Lon said. "But there's a lot more. For one thing, Charlie Meyerhoff, the managing director, has always resented Jason Remmers—feels he's a dilettante with no real knowledge of music who has his position simply because of wealth and social power."

"Mr. Remmers is the Symphony's board chairman, I believe?"

"Right, he's from the old beer family—that beer," Lon said, pointing to the bottles on Wolfe's desk. "Only he's never been much interested in the beer business, which disappointed his father. Henry Remmers must be close to eighty now, and still has active control of the firm. But Jason, who's about fifty, married society, and his wife has always been big for the arts. She's been in her glory the last few years. Actually, Jason's done a pretty fair job as chairman. It's a nonpaying post, and a big part of the role is fund-raising. He's an outgoing guy, damn popular around town, and he seems to know how to coax money out of the mattresses, because the orchestra's deficit has been cut way down."

"And he is also responsible for Mr. Stevens's move from London?" Wolfe asked.

"Absolutely. As I said, Stevens has a reputation for being tough, a real hard-nose. The Symphony had suffered from a lack of leadership and discipline, or so our music critic felt compelled to write every other Sunday."

"But Mr. Stevens hasn't been the answer?" Wolfe asked.

"Not really," Lon said, pausing for another sip of brandy. "I don't follow the Symphony like I do the Knicks, but I know there's been plenty of offstage backbiting. Both Meyerhoff and David Hirsch, the associate conductor, have been plenty open about their feelings concerning Stevens. They apparently feel—again, this is our music critic talking—that his Prussian approach hasn't worked. Oh, the orchestra has more discipline now, but at the expense of spirit. They're all so damned terrified of Stevens, or so the story goes, that the quality of the playing has fallen off. Now, I'll concede that Meyerhoff and Hirsch both have a hatchet they want to hone: Meyerhoff resents Remmers, and so probably would have criticized anyone he picked. And Hirsch wanted the job himself, from what I've heard, but doesn't have the ability to handle it."

"Is this manner of tension and infighting usual in an orchestra?" Wolfe asked as I refilled Lon's snifter and my own.

"I suppose so, to a degree," Lon answered. "Hirsch didn't get along with the last music director either, and what little I know about Meyerhoff tells me he's not exactly Mr. Sunshine. That artistic temperament you mention is justification for all kinds of behavior in the theater and music world. But the fact remains that Stevens, whatever his musical abilities, has not pulled the orchestra together the way Remmers hoped he would."

Wolfe made a face, probably envisioning wild-eyed musicians swearing at one another and throwing tantrums. He continued questioning Lon, asking about the personnel and mechanics and operation of the Symphony. Lon will always say he doesn't know much about a given subject, but invariably he turns out to be a two-legged encyclopedia on any topic you throw out. The Lon Cohen I know best seems most at home holding a pair and betting the pot, and his knowledge of the orchestra surprised even me. I could see that Wolfe was careful not to appear overly interested in Stevens, but he kept circling back to him.

Finally, at a quarter to one, Lon stretched his arms and allowed as how he had to be bright-eyed for an early-morning meeting with the publisher. "I'd kill to know what you're up to," he said, grinning at Wolfe, "but I know you aren't going to open up, so I'll just hope for the first call if something breaks. And if nothing does, I've still had the kind of evening that makes me forget we're in the midst of one of the most violent cities in the world." Lon lifted his empty glass to Wolfe and rose.

"Mr. Cohen, I appreciate your patience, and I thank you for dining with us," Wolfe said. "One more favor, if you will: Can Mr. Goodwin get access to your back files on the orchestra?"

"Consider it done," Lon said. "Archie, call before you come, and I'll clear it with our morgue." I went with Lon to the door, saw him out, and bolted it for the night, returning to the office, where Wolfe was reclining in his chair, eyes closed and fingers interlaced over his stomach.

"Okay," I said, returning to my desk, "I retract several recent comments; you really do still know how to work. But where are we? What have we got? All we really know is—"

"Archie!" It was well short of a bellow, but it stopped me. "Your notebook. Instructions."

# 5

Because I function best on at least eight hours' sleep, it was nine-thirty when I rolled out and showered, and almost ten by the time I got to the kitchen. Fritz had my copy of the *Times* propped up on the rack at the small table where I eat, and a steaming pot of coffee was ready, along with wheatcakes and bacon. I nodded to him and attacked the paper, but I could feel his eyes as I read and sipped the coffee. I finally looked up.

"Archie, how was last night?" he asked, kneading his hands. "Was the food all right? Did everything go well?"

"The tournedos were out of this world, your best work. Mr. Cohen praised them at least three times. He said it was the finest meal he'd had in years."

"Archie . . ." Fritz's dark eyes implored. "You know what I am asking you. Is he working again?"

I started in on the wheatcakes before answering. "It's possible. Even probable. I have some instructions, but I'll never be able to concentrate on them unless I can eat in peace." Fritz reddened and quickly turned away to begin working on lunch.

In fact, I did have instructions, but they were slender. Wolfe had said last night he would take the case, but only with the proviso (his word) that Maria Radovich deliver her uncle to the house for a conversation. At that point, I had accused him of trying to dodge work by setting up an impossible requirement, but he insisted that he had to see the potential victim. "Only Mr. Stevens is likely to give us an accurate accounting of who his enemies might be, at least those within the orchestra," Wolfe had said. "It is almost surely a nest of eccentrics, and no one knows them better than he. That his niece can't—or won't—be of much help has become obvious." I was also to go through the *Gazette* files on Stevens and his previous orchestral jobs and find any other information the clips might contain.

It was ten-thirty when I went to the office, opened the morning mail, and tried to call Maria with the mixed news that Wolfe would take the case—if she could deliver Uncle Milos to West Thirty-fifth Street. No answer. She was probably at a dance rehearsal, and Stevens was in his office at Symphony Hall, I supposed. I then called Lon and had better luck. He was through with his meeting and said to come on over.

"I'm still sated from last night," Lon said when I got to his office on the twentieth floor. "Please send my regards again to Fritz. Now for business: our librarian knows you're coming down to go through some clips. You can't take anything out of the morgue—house rules. But there's a photocopying machine right there. And, Archie, if something big is about to happen at the Symphony, don't forget your friends."

Ten minutes later, I was set up in the corner of a high-ceilinged dingy room with a stack of envelopes labeled "NY Symphony," one fat envelope per year, plus another, thinner envelope that read: "Stevens, Milan, NY Symph. Conduc., 1975–date."

There wasn't much in the clips that we hadn't already learned from Maria or Lon, but I was interested in the biography of Stevens that ran just after his appointment. It called him a "Yugoslav by birth" and gave his original name. It was mostly basic material: marriage and divorce, previous positions, awards, and a brief mention that his niece would be living with him in New York. The few direct quotes were general ones where he said things like "The New York Symphony is one of the world's great orchestras" and "I'm overwhelmed by the appointment." I made a photocopy of the biography, along with one of a particularly negative concert review the *Gazette* critic had done last year calling Stevens "unimaginative in his selections of music, uninspired in his leadership, and unimpressive at the podium."

Wolfe was at his desk reading and drinking beer when I walked in at five minutes to one. "There's not a lot to report," I said, replying to his questioning glance. "I've been to the *Gazette* and have some clips on Stevens." I laid them on his blotter. "Nothing exciting, except that their biography includes his given name, which must have eluded at least a few of their nine hundred thousand readers."

Wolfe wouldn't give me the satisfaction of a scowl. He spread the photocopies on his desk and began reading. After two minutes, he looked up. "Has he agreed to come?"

"I haven't gotten to Maria, or anybody else at home," I said, turning again to the phone. "I'll try again now."

"Later, after lunch," he said, hauling his bulk out of the chair and making for the dining room.

I'm sure Fritz's potato pancakes were superb, but for the second time in two days, my taste buds were on automatic pilot. When we were back in the office with coffee, I made another call to the Stevens-Radovich apartment. There was an answer this time, but not what I wanted. The maid said Maria wasn't expected home until late that night, so I left a message for her to call me—whenever she got in. "We can try going directly to Stevens," I suggested. "He's probably over at Symphony Hall right now."

Wolfe slowly set his book down, dog-earing a page. "No, Archie, our commitment is to Miss Radovich, not Mr. Stevens. Any communication with her uncle must be done through her, or with her approval."

I swiveled around, ready to argue, but the book was open and in front of his face again. After five minutes of thinking dark thoughts, I got up noisily and went to the hall, grabbing my coat from the rack and slamming the front door behind me. A light rain had begun, blending with my mood. I pulled up my collar and headed east, cooling off as I went. I was being unfair to Wolfe, I argued with myself. After all, he had agreed to take the case, although on one condition. And it was obviously going to be up to me to fulfill that condition. I turned north on Eighth Avenue and ducked into a diner where I sometimes stop for coffee. This time I ordered milk from the counterman, who had only one other customer, an old guy about six stools down who was hunched over a bowl of chili.

I took a few sips of the milk and went to the pay phone to look up the number of Maria's dance troupe, which had its studio on Forty-sixth Street in the theater district. I dialed and got a female voice, along with music in the background.

"Yes, Miss Radovich is here," the voice said, "but she's in the middle of a rehearsal right now. They should be taking a break in a few minutes." I left my name and gave her the pay-phone number. I was on the third glass of milk, with a slice of peach pie thrown in, when the phone rang. "Mr. Goodwin?" Her voice was still breathless, although this time it could have been from the dancing.

After I assured her it was me despite the different phone number, the questions started tumbling out.

"Hold it," I said. "Now catch your breath and listen while I fill you in. Mr. Wolfe says yes, he'll take your money and try to solve the problem. But you've got to do something for us."

"Yes, what is it?"

"Miss Radovich, you've got to persuade your uncle to come to Mr. Wolfe's house for a talk."

Several seconds passed, and when she spoke, she sounded desperate. "You know he won't do that—I couldn't get him to."

"Look, Miss Radovich, when you first called, I wouldn't have given a Canadian dime for our chances of waking up Mr. Wolfe. I'm happy to say I was wrong. Now he's awake, but he's also stubborn, very stubborn. He wants to see Milan Stevens in his office. Now, if you don't think you can pull it off, I'll be glad to come over, and we can talk to him together."

"No!" she replied in something between a whisper and a shout. "If you came, he would be horribly angry both with you and with me. I must get back to rehearsal now, and we practice again after dinner, so I won't be home until late, almost midnight. But then I will ask Uncle Milos. I promise you." I repeated that I'd be happy to be there for moral support, but that only rattled her more. I gave up and said I'd wait to hear.

The rain had stopped, and I needed exercise, so I walked. By the time I got home, it was a little after four, which put Wolfe in the plant rooms and meant I probably wouldn't see him again that day: I was taking Lily to the Rangers game after an early supper at Rusterman's.

If I ever decide to spend the rest of my life with one woman—a less-than-even bet—that woman will be Lily Rowan. That is, if she ever decides to spend the rest of her life with one man, and you'll have to ask her about the odds on that yourself. All of which may give you some idea about our relationship.

Lily's late father came over from Ireland and discovered that New York could use some new sewers, so he spent a lifetime building them and getting rich and powerful in the process and determining who should be elected to what office in the city and the state and sometimes Congress. Today, Lily lives in a penthouse just off Park Avenue, and at least one of her French Impressionist paintings has curators at four museums drooling.

This is fine, but more important to me are dark blue eyes and hair just a shade darker than cornsilk and the best-looking legs between Paris and Chicago, legs that are not only great to ogle, but which also move around a dance floor better than any others I've ever been with. Not to mention that each of us seems to have the other measured pretty well all the time, so nobody worries about playing parts or faking emotions.

"Escamillo, my love," Lily said over coffee after dinner, "methinks your mind is a long way from Irish colleens and hockey games. No, don't try to deny it," she said, reaching across to squeeze my arm. "Maybe it's intuition or whatever those women's magazines have taken to calling it these days, but all the way down to my toes, I have a feeling that Nero Wolfe's back at work. Or maybe it's because you've scratched your right cheek just below the ear at least four times tonight, which only happens when you're nervous, and you're only nervous when you're on a case. Of course I'd kill to know all about it, but you know damn well I'm not going to ask."

I grinned and leaned across the booth to kiss Lily's cheek—just below the right ear. "Now I see why you do so well against me when we play poker," I said. "I suppose you're going to tell me I rub my chin when I pair up or that my left eye twitches when I fill a straight?" She answered with a wink.

True to her word, Lily didn't bring up the subject of Wolfe again, and I made sure my right hand stayed away from my face. The Rangers beat Boston six-five on a short-handed goal with less than three minutes to play. We cheered as loudly as any of the seventeen thousand others in the Garden, but our enthusiasm dissolved into awkward silence as soon as we were outside.

"I'm aware," Lily said after we'd gotten a cab, "that you're a million miles away right now. I was planning to ask you in for a brandy, but if you want to take a rain check, that's fine. It wouldn't hurt me to get to bed at a decent hour for a change."

"You know of course that your knack of saying and doing precisely the right thing at the right time makes you totally irresistible to me," I said.

"Of course I know it. I've bought a table for a benefit at the Churchill two weeks from tonight, and I expect you to be my consort."

"Consider it done," I said as we pulled up to her building. I went as far as the lobby with her, and we kissed while the hallman tactfully kept his head buried in a paperback. "Take care, Escamillo," she said, easing out of my grasp and planting the tip of her finger on my nose. "I want to hear all about what you and Wolfe are up to—when you're ready to talk about it."

Back in the cab, I gave the driver a Forty-sixth Street address. About halfway through the hockey game, I'd made up my mind to try to catch Maria at her rehearsal and take her home. On the way, I hoped, I could talk her into introducing me to Uncle Milos.

My watch said eleven-fifteen when the cabbie slid to the curb in front of a brick building on a dark stretch a half-block east of Broadway. There was a stationery store at street level, with a doorway on one side with a sign above it that said "Elmar Dance Company, 2nd Floor." I walked up a long, creaky stairway, moving toward a light at the top and the sounds of what I assumed must be dance music. The stairs ended at a small reception area with a desk and a lumpy couch and dusty photographs of dancers hanging at cockeyed angles on the walls. A hallway led farther back, to where the music was coming from.

Just as I started in the direction of the sound, a tall blonde with lots of eye makeup and an overnight case popped out of a doorway about halfway down, obviously on her way out.

"Hi, who you lookin' for?" she asked, showing a mouthful of teeth that deserved to be in a chewing-gum ad. When I answered, she said Maria was changing. "Why don't you take a seat? She's got to pass you to get out of here."

Three more dancers, two of them lookers, sailed by chattering before Maria came out, wearing slacks and with her hair tied back in a scarf. She saw me and stopped, but before she could say anything, I was up and smiling.

"The more I thought about it, the more I felt I should take you home tonight. Come on, we can get a cab over on Broadway. And on the way, I'll tell you why we should see your uncle together."

Maria frowned and shook her head. "No, I've told you he won't talk to you when he finds out why you've come. Please, I promised on the telephone that I'd ask him tonight about seeing Mr. Wolfe."

Walking to Broadway and then on the cab ride north, I kept pressing Maria, but whatever charm Wolfe thinks I have with women wasn't working on this one. Her one concession was to let me come into the building with her, but only as far as the lobby. I would wait there while she went up to talk to her uncle. Then, if she needed reinforcements, she'd call down for me. I wasn't wild about the plan, because Stefanovic didn't sound like the type to let his niece talk him into a damn thing. But I wasn't getting a choice.

The cab squealed to a stop in front of an undistinguished brick building in the first block east of Park. I was expecting a little more class, at least a doorman, but this place looked like dozens of other fifty-year-old buildings in the area. I paid the driver, and we went into a small, dimly lit lobby. "Tom, this is Mr. Goodwin; he's going to wait for me here," Maria said to the hallman, a young, weak-chinned guy who looked up from behind the counter and nodded. "I'll come down or call down for him in a few minutes."

I hope so, I thought as she went up in the elevator. I plopped down on one of the dark red sofas and started thumbing through a magazine that was on the coffee table. No more than two minutes had passed when the phone at the front desk rang. "Mr. Goodwin, Miss Radovich wants you to go on up," Tom said. "It's the ninth floor, the door to your right as you get off the elevator. You can't miss it; there're only two apartments to the floor."

Either Uncle Milos wasn't home or Maria had gotten some fast results one way or the other. Ready for the worst, I tried to prepare an approach to him as the automatic elevator growled its way up to nine. But I wasn't prepared for what I saw when the doors opened.

Maria was standing in the doorway of the apartment, or more correctly, leaning against one side of it. Her eyes were open wide, but she barely acknowledged me. I put an arm around her for support as her legs began to fold up. "On the floor . . ." she said, covering her face with her hands. "Dead, dead, dead . . ."

## 6

I got Maria inside and shut the door. We were in an entrance hall that had a chandelier and a handsome Oriental rug. I led her to a chair and eased her down as the sobs started. "Where?" I asked. She pointed to an open door at the far end of the hall. "Stay here," I said. "Don't try to move."

The doorway led into a good-sized library with a high ceiling, fireplace, dark paneling, lots of bookshelves, a grand piano, and another Oriental rug, a Kashan. The body was lying facedown on the rug in one corner near a high monk-style writing desk that had a stool behind it. I knelt and made a quick check, but Maria had been right. Milan Stevens was dead, and it wasn't hard to figure out why: The back of his white shirt was torn and stained dark red, and a fancy long-handled letter opener, one of those made to look like a sword, lay a few feet away. The blood on the opener glistened in the light, and from the look of Stevens's shirt, that little sword had been run in and out of him several times.

I tried to freeze the scene in my mind, but there wasn't much to freeze. None of the furniture appeared out of place, and there was no indication of a struggle. A softcover book lay open on the monk's desk, and I covered my hand with my handkerchief as I turned the pages. It was music, plus a lot of penciled notations that might as well have been in Urdu. For the record, the cover sheet of the music said "Symphony No. 4 in E minor, for Orchestra, by Johannes Brahms, Op. 98."

I went back to the hall, where Maria was still sitting. She'd stopped crying and now was staring straight ahead. "He is dead, isn't he?" she asked, blinking.

"Yes. Now listen carefully; I'm going to have to call the police, and I have to do it soon. When they come, tell them everything about the notes, about going to see Mr. Wolfe, all of it. But first, I have two things to do. Please stay right here." She nodded, but otherwise there was no reaction or expression. Shock was settling in.

I went back to the study and, using the handkerchief again, dialed the number I know best. Wolfe answered after one ring.

"The notes must have been for real," I said. "Stevens is dead. Stabbed in his study. I'm there now, with Maria, and I'm about to call the police. Instructions?"

I could hear him draw in air and let it out slowly. "No," he said. "I suppose you'll have to go to headquarters?"

"Without question," I said. "And I've told Maria not to keep anything from them. I figure it's going to be a long night. I'll report first thing in the morning, if they let me out by then."

"Very well," Wolfe said with disgust. "Have you eaten?" I assured him that Rusterman's lamb chops would carry me through the night, and I went back to Maria. She hadn't moved and gave me another mechanical nod when I told her I was going to the lobby for a couple of minutes.

Tom was still behind the counter. "Excuse me," I said with what I hoped was a friendly smile. "Did Mr. Stevens have any guests earlier this evening, before Miss Radovich and I got here?"

He looked up with a slightly amused expression. "Why don't you ask him yourself?"

"He's asleep," I said. "And Miss Radovich had been expecting a visitor. She wondered if anyone had come by."

Tom was sizing me up, trying to decide whether or not I was okay, and he finally made up his mind. "Well . . . there was one," he said. "His name was Milner, or something like that. He came in about eight-fifteen, but didn't stay long—maybe five minutes."

"His first name?" I asked.

"Didn't leave one. I just called upstairs to Mr. Stevens and told him Mr. Milner was here, and he said to send him up."

"Did Mr. Milner say anything to you when he left?"

"Nope. Just walked on out. All I saw was his back going through the lobby."

"And he was the only caller?"

"Yeah."

"Thanks, Tom," I said. "You've leveled with me, and now I'd better tell you something. Mr. Stevens is dead—killed. The police will be here soon."

I watched his face closely, and got the predictable openmouthed, wide-eyed look. "What? Hey, why didn't you say that right away?" He jumped up, knocking his chair over. He looked scared. "I can't tell them anything," he said, swallowing hard. "It must have been that Milner guy, huh? What should I do when they come?"

"Take it easy," I said. "They'll want to know just what you told me. About Mr. Milner, about anything else the Symphony a couple of years or so. But I've talked to him on occasion at receptions and such—I try to make it a point to meet everyone in the orchestra—and it's difficult for me to picture him being even the least bit scheming, let alone violent. The orchestra is made up of a great many disparate personalities, as you can appreciate, and his is among the mildest—perhaps 'meekest' is a better word—of them all."

"The meek and mild have wreaked a great deal of destruction through the ages," Wolfe said.

"Certainly, and it may indeed be that Milner is one of those," Remmers conceded. "But I simply don't believe it."

"Do you have someone else to suggest?"

"I've been doing a lot of thinking about it. There were a number of people who found it, well . . . *difficult* to get along with Milan Stevens. He was rigid and unbending, as you probably have heard, and a lot of people who had to work with him were put off by his attitude and personality."

"Including you?"

"I guess I was a special case. I brought him here from London two years ago—two-and-a-half, actually—and he felt a debt to me because of that. Besides, as chairman I don't get very involved in the day-to-day operations of the orchestra, so Stevens and I didn't really have occasion to clash."

"But he collided with others at a high level?"

Remmers smiled ruefully. "Yes, indeed. For instance, he and Charles Meyerhoff, the managing director, were openly hostile to each other. Charlie felt the orchestra's morale was even worse than it had been under the previous conductor, and that the choice of repertoire made us seem like a glorified Boston Pops."

Wolfe looked puzzled, and Remmers picked up on it. "That is, under Stevens, the Symphony was playing music that appealed to the greatest numbers, rather than music that was necessarily of the highest caliber, or music that was more adventuresome."

"Was this true?"

"That's a subjective judgment," Remmers answered, "although there's no question that the Symphony programs the last two seasons have run more heavily toward Tchaikovsky, Rachmaninoff, Beethoven, Brahms, and so forth, the popular composers."

"Did you agree with Mr. Meyerhoff's position on the orchestra's morale?" Wolfe asked.

"Not at first," Remmers said. "Charlie tends to be a griper by nature—never satisfied, never happy. So when he initially came to me complaining about Stevens's Prussian approach, I shrugged it off as just another example of his pessimistic outlook. Besides, one of the big reasons we brought Milan in was to reestablish discipline in the orchestra. For a number of years, the Symphony had been without a strong music director, and this was reflected in the quality of the playing. At first, I was delighted to hear about the new strictness."

"But your opinion changed?"

"Yes," Remmers said. "After the first year, I began to realize that Milan was alienating a number of people with his approach, and during the second year, it seemed as if almost everyone was being alienated by his policies, his brusqueness, his inflexibility."

"Did you talk to him about this?" Wolfe asked.

"Lord, yes, numerous times. I tried to explain that we needed discipline without intimidation, and he would always insist that this was his way of operating, that it had been successful in London, Vienna, and other places. But each time, our conversations ended with him saying he would try to be more understanding and easier to get along with.

"Unfortunately, his good intentions never seemed to last long, and Meyerhoff would be back griping to me. In the last few months, Charlie started saying he was going to quit, that he couldn't take the fighting and tension and what he felt was the overpopularization of the repertoire. He said he couldn't function when we had a music director who wanted to be the general manager as well."

"But you were able to keep Mr. Meyerhoff in the fold?" Wolfe asked.

"Barely. For the last eight months or so, my main function has been peacemaker, rather than fund-raiser and civic representative of the Symphony, which is what I'm supposed to be. It's been rough," he said, running a hand across his chin.

"Are you suggesting by all this that Mr. Meyerhoff might have killed Milan Stevens?"

Remmers jerked upright. "Oh no, no, not necessarily. There were others who probably disliked Milan every bit as much as he did. To name two, Dave Hirsch, the associate conductor, and Donald Sommers, the principal flutist."

Wolfe shifted uneasily. He hadn't rung for beer, and I knew why. "What were the causes of their animus toward Mr. Stevens?"

"Well, Hirsch had been associate conductor under the previous music director and seemed to think he was the logical choice at the time we brought in Stevens. But it was explained to him that he wasn't even being considered for the post. Off the record, he just hasn't got the presence or the depth for the job. Anyway, he's resented Stevens from day one, and it's gotten worse. Milan didn't delegate much responsibility, so Hirsch was doing less than he had before. And to make matters worse, Hirsch had composed a symphony that he would dearly love to have premiered by the orchestra. But Stevens told him he didn't find its caliber high enough for the Symphony. Since then, they've barely been on speaking terms. I've been expecting Hirsch to come in any day and tell me he's quitting after the current season."

"With Mr. Stevens dead, will Mr. Hirsch become the music director?" Wolfe asked.

Remmers shook his head vigorously. "Only on an interim basis. We're making the formal announcement of his appointment this afternoon. I've already talked to Dave, and he seems resigned to never being the Symphony's chief conductor. Down deep, I think he's aware of his limitations, and he knows he could never handle the job in the long run. I suspect he realizes that any potential he has for growth in the music world is as a composer rather than a conductor.

"In fact, part of my peacemaking work in the last few weeks was trying to persuade Stevens to give the premiere of Hirsch's symphony. And I think I just about talked him into it."

Wolfe considered the wall clock, then looked back at Remmers. "And what of Mr. Sommers?"

"Ah yes, another case of bitterness," he said. "Don Sommers performed a flute solo a few weeks ago that got so-so reviews, and not long afterward, in an interview in the *Times*, Stevens said one of his biggest problems was the lackadaisical attitude of a number of the principal players. Sommers chose to interpret this as a direct slap at him, although in the paper Stevens was quoted as criticizing 'several soloists.' Anyway, the two of them got into a shouting session backstage a day or two later, and since then, they hadn't been on speaking terms."

Wolfe frowned. "It would seem that the orchestra exists on a continuum of screaming matches and angry silences."

Remmers threw back his head and laughed. "Based on what I've told you, that's a natural enough conclusion. Actually, though, things aren't nearly that chaotic most of the time. But then, you asked specifically about those people who had problems with Milan Stevens, so you're hearing about the turmoil."

"What I started out asking for," Wolfe corrected, "were your suggestions as to who might have killed Mr. Stevens. Do you think any of the three you named—or anyone else within the orchestra—is a likely candidate?"

"A few days ago, I would have laughed off that question. But a few days ago, I'd also have scoffed at anyone who said that our music director would be stabbed to death in his own home. To be totally candid, I wouldn't rule out any of them, although I wouldn't presume to point at one as a more likely suspect than the other two. As far as the rest of the orchestra . . . no, these three and Milner were the only ones I'm aware of who've had particularly bitter experiences with Stevens."

Wolfe scowled. "Let's return to you, sir. Because you were instrumental in the hiring of Mr. Stevens, has some of the criticism of his performance been directed to you?"

"Indeed it has," Remmers said. "One paper's music critic has said that the blame for what he called the 'Stevens debacle' should rest with me. You see, at the time we were looking for a new music director, the music-policy committee was terribly split on candidates for the job. Meyerhoff is head of that committee, but they were going nowhere, so I stepped in with Stevens's name. I got support for him from committee members, and finally Meyerhoff gave in too. In recent months, some of the same people on the committee who applauded that selection began saying I made a first-class blunder."

"What has your response been to this criticism?"

"I'm pretty thick-skinned, Mr. Wolfe," he said, coming on again with that engaging grin that you see in society-page photographs. "I've been involved in a number of civic projects through the years, and I've taken a lot of shots from a lot of people because of various decisions of mine. All of which has helped me grow a tough hide. The only thing that's bothered me about the flap over Stevens is the realization I've come to in the last six months: Stevens wasn't working out. I *had* made a bum call, and I was prepared to rectify it."

"Were you planning to fire him?" Wolfe asked.

"In effect. His contract was up for renewal, and I was going before the board with the suggestion that we seek a new music director."

"Was Mr. Stevens aware of this?"

"I hadn't talked to him about it, although I would have in the next few weeks," Remmers said. "I think he probably suspected it might be coming, though."

"Would you have taken this as a personal failure?" Wolfe asked.

Remmers shrugged his lean shoulders. "Not really. Again, I'm used to criticism—you can't have a position like this one without being a target. And considering the problems the Symphony had with its last few conductors, Stevens really wasn't that much of a disaster."

"Mr. Remmers, if I may shift to another subject," Wolfe said, "do you know a woman named Lucinda Forrester-Moore?"

"I suppose you could say I know her," Remmers said. "I've met her at a number of parties, benefits, that sort of thing, through the years. Her late husband, Baxter Moore, and I both went to Harvard, and we ran into each other at alumni functions; he was in the shipping business. I guess I know why you're asking about her: She and Milan Stevens had become an item in the last year or so."

"Did you perceive theirs as a serious relationship?" Wolfe asked.

"I couldn't really say. They were together a good deal, of course, but I could never figure out whether it was romantic or just a handy pairing. Lucinda loves to be in the middle of things, and it's pretty damn prestigious to have the Symphony maestro on your arm when you sweep into the theater or a dinner party. But then, since her husband's death six, seven years ago, she's had a history of attracting well-known men—it's sort of her trademark."

"Did Mr. Stevens ever mention her to you?"

"No, I don't think so," Remmers said. "However, there was no particular reason why he should. Our own relationship wasn't such that personal matters were discussed. In fact, I can't picture Milan Stevens discussing his personal life with anybody."

Wolfe drew in half the oxygen in the room, then exhaled slowly. "Just two more questions, Mr. Remmers. First, if I want to see the three men you mentioned, could you arrange it?"

"Yes, I think so. You'd want to see them here, of course. They might not like it, particularly Charlie Meyerhoff, but they'll come, either together or separately, as you wish. If you let me know when you want them . . ."

"Mr. Goodwin will call you with a precise time," Wolfe said. "And we'll want to see them all at once. The other question, sir: Where were you on Wednesday night between seven-thirty and eight-thirty?"

Remmers flashed that grin again. It was easy to see him in the role of fund-raiser. "I knew that was coming. Nineteen nights out of twenty, I'd have a drum-tight alibi—a dinner, a reception, the opera, maybe the Symphony itself. But I had an upset stomach Wednesday, so I begged off a dinner invitation at the home of some friends, and my wife went alone. I spent the early part of the evening reading, and about a quarter to eight, I went out for a walk—I needed the fresh air to help settle me. I walked around a few blocks in our neighborhood—we live on Beekman Place—and I was back home by nine or so. Unfortunate timing, isn't it?"

"Did you see anyone?" Wolfe asked.

"Just the doorman in our building, and I suppose the hallman, too. The doorman and I chatted briefly both when I left and came back. Otherwise, I saw at least a dozen people walking their dogs, but nobody I knew."

"Very well," Wolfe said, looking at the wall clock again. "I know your schedule is a busy one, and I appreciate your taking the time to come here."

"Thank *you,* Mr. Wolfe," Remmers said, rising. He started to reach out a hand, then remembered where he was and dipped his head. I followed him out to the front hall and helped him on with the cashmere, then watched him bound down the steps to a parked limousine that looked to be twice the length of the car that had waited for Cramer earlier.

When I got back to the office, Fritz was on his way out, having just deposited a glass and two bottles of beer in front of Wolfe. "Hah!" I said. "You didn't want him to see you drinking the family brew, did you? Afraid he'd think you were buttering him up?"

"Nonsense," Wolfe shot back as he poured beer and watched the foam settle. "It merely would have distracted from our conversation. Mr. Remmers undoubtedly would have felt some comment was necessary, which in turn would have elicited a response from me, and so on. I did not invite him here to indulge in small talk."

"You didn't invite him at all, he invited himself," I retorted, but his face was already hidden by an open book, which always happens when I get in the last word.

## 13

I'm sure Fritz's poached salmon with mousse-line d'homard was superb, but for the third straight day I was eating without tasting. I envy Wolfe's facility for totally shutting out business whenever he crosses the sill into the dining room; that afternoon he put away three big helpings of the salmon, all the while holding forth on how future historians might view the presidency of one Richard M. Nixon. I threw in a few comments here and there, but on balance I was hardly a good conversational partner. As strong as my own feelings are about the man from San Clemente, I couldn't get my mind off Maria Radovich and Jason Remmers and Gerald Milner, the last of whom was at that very moment sitting in the South Room eating the same food we were.

It seemed as if lunch lasted six hours, but finally we were back in the office with coffee, which meant business was fair game again. "Look," I said, swiveling in my chair to face Wolfe, "how long are we going to keep our houseguest? I can't see that he's doing us any good here."

Wolfe sipped his coffee and set the cup down deliberately. "I agree that the time has come to turn Mr. Milner loose. My principal reason for housing him was to give Mr. Cohen and his newspaper an advantage over their competition on the story. They now have that advantage, so he should be told that he is free to go."

What Wolfe was actually saying was that I should suggest to Milner that he pack. Heaven forbid that Wolfe himself have to tell a guest to leave. I was about to make a remark when the doorbell rang.

"Probably Cramer," I said, "back again to try talking us off the case. Are you available?"

He grunted. "Yes, I'll see him."

But it wasn't the inspector's mug I saw when I looked through the one-way panel. I wouldn't have wanted to try guessing her age, although her well-coiffed white hair told me she'd already been around awhile when I first saw the light of day back in Ohio. Her skin looked as good as a teenager's, though, and if pressed for a single adjective, I would have called her elegant. She was wearing a black coat with a white fur collar that had to have set her back a few bills. Whoever she was, I concluded she was no immediate threat, so I slid off the chain lock.

"Yes?" I said, swinging open the door.

"I would like to see Mr. Wolfe," she said. "I realize I don't have an appointment, but I know he is at home most of the time." Her voice seemed tinged with French, although as Wolfe has pointed out a number of times, I'm out of my league when it comes to languages and accents.

"I don't know if he can be disturbed right now," I said, stepping back and letting her in so I could close the door against the November gusts. "I'll ask, though. Who should I say is calling?"

"My name is Alexandra Adjari," she said.

It registered, of course, and I turned toward the open door to the office. When I got there, Wolfe was on his feet, looking past me into the hall with an expression I'd never seen him wear. I was trying to read it when she eased past me. "Hello, Nero, it's been a long time," she said, holding out a gloved hand.

"Alexandra," he answered, shaking hands across the desk. "I recognized your voice instantly."

"Even though you hadn't heard it in heaven knows how many years?" she said with a laugh. A nice laugh. "I don't believe you, Nero, but thank you for saying it. You're looking well."

Wolfe gestured at himself. "As you can see, I've added layers through the years—insulation against life's myriad assaults." He turned toward me. "This is Mr. Goodwin."

She took my hand with a firm grasp and smiled. "I assumed so when I saw him at the door. I've read a good deal about both of you through the years. I see the New York *Times* frequently."

Wolfe dipped his head a full inch, which is for him a sweeping bow. "Please," he said, indicating the red leather chair. I took her coat and hung it up, and when I got back, he was asking if she'd eaten.

"Yes, thank you, I had lunch on the plane coming over. I've only just been in New York an hour or so. I started making arrangements to come as soon as I heard about Milos. As you can imagine, it's big news in London, too."

Wolfe nodded, and at his suggestion, Alexandra agreed to have coffee. After Fritz had served her and she'd taken a first sip, he readjusted himself and dabbed the corner of his mouth with a handkerchief. "You've come for the memorial services?"

"Partly," she said, "but also to be with Maria Radovich. I'm very fond of her, and I thought she might need some comforting, having no relatives other than Milos. I tried to call her after I checked in at the Churchill, but there was no answer at their apartment."

"Mr. Goodwin knows her whereabouts," Wolfe said, "and can tell you how to reach her. I can assure you she's in the care of friendly and sympathetic persons. As far as memorial arrangements, details are not yet firm."

Alexandra waved her hand. "That's not my main concern," she said. "Let the dead bury their dead. I know that must sound callous, considering that I was married to the man for seventeen years, but as I think you know, it was a marriage in name only after the first three years or so. We were separated the rest of the time, and we were divorced . . ."—she paused to think—". . . more years ago than I care to remember. I don't think I've even seen Milos more than four or five times in all the years since then. I can still remember what you told me after I decided to marry him—can you?"

Wolfe nodded and took another sip of coffee.

She went on. "You said we wouldn't last five years together, and that I should reconsider. In the early months after the wedding, I laughed to myself about that, thinking how wrong you were. But by the end of that first year, I knew what a mistake we'd made, how totally unsuited we were to each other. When I was with him constantly over a long period of time, I found that Milos was hard to love, harder still to like. Fortunately, his music took him away so frequently that we stayed together longer than we would have otherwise. Even at that, the marriage was an almost total disaster. The only good things I can think of were that we didn't have any children and that because of Milos, I came to know Maria."

She paused for some coffee. "Long after we divorced, Milos came to London as conductor of the Philharmonia, and I met him at a reception. We were polite to each other, and he introduced me to Maria, who was then about thirteen. I liked her right away, and she seemed fond of me, too. I know Milos tried to discourage her from being friendly with me, at least at first, but Maria has her own mind, and we grew close over the next several years. Since she moved here with Milos, we write to each other only occasionally, but I still think of her often. It's because of Maria that I came. Now that I'm here, though, I find another purpose: In my room at the hotel was a copy of today's New York *Gazette*, and it said that you're investigating Milos's murder, that you're not satisfied the right man has been arrested. Is that correct?"

"It is," Wolfe said.

"The newspaper also said you're acting on Maria's behalf."

"Also true," Wolfe said. "I'm sure she'll tell you as much when you meet."

"I have never met her beau, of course, but I suppose it's natural she would think him innocent. You must also be convinced of his innocence." It was a statement, not a question.

"I am," Wolfe said, "although I can offer no other candidate at the present time."

"I'm sure your reasons are good. I know Maria has limited funds of her own, at least until the estate is settled, but I have no such constraint. Nero, I want to employ you to find Milos's murderer, and you may set whatever fee you wish."

I looked at Wolfe. We already had a client, albeit one whose assets would hardly qualify her as a preferred customer at Metropolitan Trust. But in the last few hours, two heavy hitters had stepped up and asked to join the team. I waited for his answer, although I knew what it would be.

"I appreciate the offer, but—"

"I know, you're wondering why I would do this for a

man for whom I had no feelings all these years. I suppose it's because of Maria, and because he *was* my husband once. And perhaps because of my own conscience. I was as much the cause of the marriage's failure as he."

"What I started to say," Wolfe replied, "was that I appreciate the offer, but even Miss Radovich is only a token client. As you well know, I owe Milos Stefanovic my life."

She nodded and looked thoughtful. "Yes, that day in Cetinje, the police, the blockade . . ."

"I was a consummate fool," Wolfe said. "I made every possible mistake, but Milos appeared from somewhere with a rifle and a pistol. He must have killed three of them."

"Five, he said, when he told me the story later. But I seem to recall that you saved him at least once also, Nero."

Wolfe turned a palm over. "I suppose one could say we all saved each other on numerous occasions. But nothing as marked as what happened that afternoon. It is a debt, and I dislike being in debt."

"You've changed very little," Alexandra said, smiling again. "Even then, you hated owing anything to anyone. Well, if you won't take my money, you certainly have my moral support, for what that's worth."

"Thank you," Wolfe said, bowing again. I was beginning to get worried about him. Three times this week he had stood when women entered or left the office, if you count twice for Maria, and I'd lost track of the number of times he'd bowed. If this trend kept up, he'd soon start helping women on with their coats or opening the front door for them.

"Nero," Alexandra said, "I've come to New York a number of times through the years, and I've often thought of calling or stopping by. For some reason, I never did, but I always told myself I would one day.

And I promised myself that when I did, I would ask to see those famous orchids. Is that presumptuous?"

Wolfe raised his eyebrows. "Presumptuous? Quite the contrary. Mr. Goodwin will tell you that I rarely deny that request. If you feel rested, we can go now," he said, lifting himself from the chair.

"I certainly do," she replied, and they made for the hall. "You'll stay for dinner, of course," Wolfe asked.

"I'd like that, if it's no imposition," Alexandra replied.

"In this house, a meal is always—" The rest of Wolfe's sentence was chopped off by the closing of the elevator door.

I sat back down in my chair and stared at the wall. She and Wolfe went back a long way, and the relationship obviously hadn't been a casual one. Well, I'll be damned, I said to myself, or maybe it was out loud. I thought I had long ago learned everything I was going to know about Nero Wolfe, but here was something new. I smiled and started in on some of the office work that had been piling up.

I'd been at it about ten minutes when the phone rang. It was Wolfe, from the plant rooms. "I wanted to remind you that Mr. Milner is free to go, and indeed, he'd probably like to leave soon so he can visit Miss Radovich. Also, I know you see Saul regularly to play cards. What about Fred—is he still working?"

"Yes, or at least he's trying. Bascomb uses him once in a while, but I know things have been slow for him."

"Can you have both of them here tomorrow, say, at eleven?"

"I can certainly try," I said. "And by the way, I may have forgotten to mention that I'm dining at Miss Rowan's tonight."

"Satisfactory," he said, hanging up.

I allowed myself another grin. You may think the "satisfactory" was in response to my trying to deliver a pair of men to the office the next morning, but it was really his reaction to knowing there would be only two at the dinner table in the brownstone. And for the record, I didn't have a date at Lily Rowan's, although I was pretty sure I could wangle one. While I was at it, maybe I could hook an invite for Milner as well, since there was a certain party at Lily's that he wanted to see. I turned back to the phone.

## 14

At eleven o'clock on Saturday morning, Nero Wolfe stepped out of the elevator that had lowered him from the plant rooms and walked into his office to find the three of us waiting: Saul Panzer in the red leather chair, Fred Durkin in one of the yellow chairs, me at my desk. They stood when he came in, and he stopped to shake hands with both of them—something he reserves for perhaps a dozen men. He then circled behind his desk, sat, and rang for beer.

Pretty cool, I thought. He hasn't seen them in close to two years, but he's acting like they were over for dinner yesterday. In case you're new in these precincts, Saul and Fred were free-lancing for Wolfe long before the Giants and Dodgers snuck off to California. About Saul Panzer: He's short, his face is mostly nose, his clothes are rumpled, and he always looks like he hasn't shaved for three days, although he insists he takes a blade to his mug every morning. But he's hands down the finest operative, free-lance or otherwise, in the city of New York, when it comes to tailing someone or sniffing out clues or persuading people to spit out information they'd rather keep to themselves. Saul asks for, and gets, double the going rate, and he never hurts for business, although through the years he's always been willing to rearrange his schedule for Wolfe.

Fred Durkin is a big guy, thick at the waist, thick at the neck, and maybe a little thick upstairs, too, although he's almost as good as Saul at tailing, and he's as honest and loyal as you'll ever find. But as I had told Wolfe, Fred wasn't getting much work these days. Fortunately, his wife, Fanny, had a job at a branch library someplace out on Long Island, so at least a little money was coming in.

But I've gotten a bit ahead of myself, so I'll back up to yesterday afternoon. The moment Wolfe and Alexandra went up to the plant rooms, I was on the phone. I got Saul on the first try, which surprised me, and when I told him Wolfe wanted to see him, he said: "The Stevens thing; I'll be there." That's Saul. Fred was home too, and from the tone of his voice, I knew he'd crawl across Manhattan for a job, especially with Wolfe. He'd be there too. Next came a call to Lily. I landed that dinner invitation, all right, for both Milner and me, so his short stay as our houseguest was over, and I could have back the clothes of mine that he'd been wearing for the last day or so, and which were about two sizes too large for him. Actually, he hadn't been much of an imposition to us, as he'd almost never come out of the South Room, which may be a tribute to the high quality of the books on the shelves up there.

As he and I rode to Lily's in a cab, Milner was quiet but didn't seem terribly worried, or terribly curious about our progress, for that matter. When I asked why, he said, "I didn't do it, and I know Mr. Wolfe's reputation. I'm just thankful he's working on this, because I know he'll find the right one." I wish I were that confident, I thought, slouching in the seat and staring out at the snowflakes swirling in the wind.

Maria was still staying at Lily's, and she seemed brightened by Milner's appearance, although she was preoccupied with plans for a memorial service for her uncle, which was set for Monday. She brightened further when I told her Alexandra Adjari was in town and would be calling her either that night or the next morning. As it turned out, Alexandra went one better, stopping off at Lily's about ten-thirty on her way from the brownstone to her hotel, and the two had a tears-and-hugs reunion right there in the living room. It ended up with Alexandra insisting that Maria stay with her at the Churchill, which meant Lily was losing her houseguest, too. The two women and Milner left in a cab—he had decided to go back to his apartment in Queens—and all of a sudden, Lily and I had her palace to ourselves. That's a whole story in itself, and not for these pages, but now you're up-to-date on Friday night's developments.

When Fritz brought Wolfe's beer, he took orders from the rest of us: coffee for Saul and me, and beer for Fred, who doesn't like it that much but thinks he should drink it when he's with Wolfe, to be sociable. After everyone was served, Wolfe's eyes moved from Saul to Fred and back again. We were all a touch uneasy, I think, as it was the first time we'd been together in this room since Orrie had blown himself up on the front stoop. In the past, Saul, Fred, and Orrie had almost always come as a group for instructions, and the empty yellow chair was on all our minds.

Wolfe set his glass down and began: "You both read the papers regularly, so you no doubt know I'm involved in a case." They nodded. "You also know then that Milos Stefanovic, or Milan Stevens as he called himself, was a Montenegrin whom I had known many years ago in Europe. In addition, the papers have reported, correctly, that I do not believe Stefanovic was killed by Gerald Milner." Wolfe proceeded to fill them in on the last few days' activities, asking me several times to insert first-person narrative, such as when I went into the Stevens library and saw the body. When he had finished, he poured more beer and watched the foam settle. "Before the weekend is over," he said, "I hope to talk to Messrs. Meyerhoff, Hirsch, and Sommers of the Symphony, if Archie can get them here. Archie also is going to visit Mrs. Forrester-Moore at her home—she was a frequent companion of Mr. Stevens's in the last few months." I glared at Wolfe, who ignored me and went on.

"Saul, go to the building where Stevens lived. Find some pretense to get inside. I'd like to know how many entrances there are, and how easy it would be to enter and leave without being seen by the hallman. Is there a fire escape? A back stairway? A service elevator?" I smiled and bit my lip. Wolfe was out of practice, because these were questions Saul would answer without being asked. If I knew him, he'd bring back a blueprint of the whole place, complete with heating ducts and wiring.

Wolfe shifted his glance. "Fred, learn what you can about the hallman who was on duty that night, his name is—" He turned to me. "Tom Hubbard," I said. "Find out what you can about Mr. Hubbard and his habits, but don't talk to him, at least not yet. The police have surely questioned him thoroughly, and he'll be on his guard."

As Wolfe talked, Fred was scribbling in a pocket notebook, unlike Saul, who never takes any notes but keeps everything filed away upstairs. When Wolfe had finished with his briefing, the two of them got up, businesslike as usual, and shook hands again with him. It was almost like old times as I walked to the front hall with them.

"Write when you have time, even if it's only a postcard," I said as they started out the door.

"Good luck with the society doll," Saul retorted, winking. "Understand she's quite a babe. Can you handle it?" I silently mouthed a word and slammed the door behind them.

Back in the office, Wolfe had picked up a book, *In Praise of English*, by Joseph T. Shipley. I sat at my desk and swiveled to face him. "Thanks so much for filling me in on my assignments," I said. "I always appreciate getting orders in front of company."

Wolfe put down the book and raised his eyebrows. "Indeed? Fred and Saul company? You're the one who once said they're part of the family, and I agree. Further, I hadn't decided who was going to do what until you were all sitting here."

"Hah! Who else but me would you send to see an attractive woman?"

He didn't reply, and I couldn't see his expression because the open book was in the way. After about five minutes, I exhaled loudly and deeply. "Okay, what do you want done first, Lucinda or the three from the Symphony?"

"Try to see the lady as soon as possible," came the voice from behind the book. "As for the others, tomorrow afternoon will be soon enough. Mr. Remmers can be of some help there."

"Any special instructions regarding the woman with the hyphenated name?" I asked.

"Use your intelligence guided by experience," Wolfe said, still behind the book. It was a favorite line of his.

"Consider it done," I said, getting up to go to the kitchen for a glass of milk. I was afraid that if I stayed in the same room with him for another thirty seconds, I might do something natural, such as braining him with his ebony paperweight.

## 15

I considered calling first, but decided my chances of seeing her might be better if I just showed up. I put on my best suit, a gray glen plaid, along with a light blue shirt and a blue-and-red paisley tie that Lily says makes me look debonair. Not bad, I told the mirror before giving my hair one more swipe with a brush. It was two-twenty when I grabbed my coat from the hall rack. Wolfe was back at his desk, reading. During lunch, I hadn't been very talkative, partly because I was still sore at him and partly because I was thinking about how to approach one of the town's reigning social lionesses.

Lucinda Forrester-Moore isn't listed in the Manhattan telephone directory, but Lily has some sort of guide to the city's elite, and when I called her, she looked up the address, which turned out to be a building about two blocks up Park from her own place. That was too long a walk on too cold a day, so I took a cab. The driver pulled up in front of one of those tall white modern buildings that have so many setbacks they look like squared-off wedding cakes, a style which if nothing else provides terraces for a lot of the upper-altitude apartments. A doorman who still had his uniform from Napoleon's army sniffed as I passed him, and I found myself in a circular lobby that was all floor-to-ceiling mirrors. There was an alcove at the far side of the circle where a hallman in a pretty snappy uniform of his own sat behind a desk. He looked up as I approached, but didn't open his mouth.

"I'd like to see Mrs. Forrester-Moore," I said. "My name is Archie Goodwin." I gave him my top-of-the-line calling card, a glossy eggshell-white job with my name engraved in the center and the words "Office of Nero Wolfe" in the lower right-hand corner. "Is she expecting you?" he asked in a bored tone that he probably practiced evenings at home.

"No, but I think she'll want to see me. When you call upstairs, make sure you mention that I'm from Nero Wolfe's office," I said, trying to sound bored myself.

He turned to his white telephone and punched out a number. He kept his voice so low I couldn't hear him from three feet away, and after a few seconds he hung up and turned back to me.

"She'll see you," he said, wearing the disappointment all over his face. "Sixteenth floor." He pointed to the elevators in a hallway off the circle. A young kid in a not-so-fancy uniform ran me up to sixteen in silence, and as the doors opened, he pointed to the left. "That's the door you go to," he said. "Only apartment on the floor."

When I pressed the buzzer, I didn't hear anything ring, but after a few seconds the door swung open to reveal a mousy little woman in a black-and-white uniform with a starched cap. "Mr. Goodwin?" she asked. When I nodded she slid to one side in a classic maid's motion so I could pass. I was in an entrance hall the size of a small church, with a chandelier that looked as if it could light Madison Square Garden. "Please wait in here," the maid said, leading me to a sitting room with a white rug, white walls, and white furniture. "Mrs. Forrester-Moore asked me to tell you she'll join you shortly."

"Shortly" turned out to be twenty-four minutes by the digital watch Lily had given me for my birthday. I was on the second cigarette when she walked in and held out a manicured hand. "Mr. Goodwin. This *is* a nice surprise," she said. "I hope you'll pardon the wait; I was napping when you rang and . . ." She smiled and gestured at her clothes and her hair. Even at fifty-plus, Lucinda Forrester-Moore was easy to look at. She was wearing a floor-length yellow-and-orange flowered number with ruffles on the cuffs and collar, and her dusty-blond hair looked like the handiwork of a gilt-edged Fifth Avenue salon.

"Please sit down," she said with a slight trace of some kind of accent. This was my week for foreign women. "Can I get you a drink?" she asked as she sat in a chair across the coffee table from mine.

I said no and began to state my business, when she interrupted. "I've heard and read about you before, of course, but haven't we met somewhere? I should remember, but I can't."

"You've got a good memory at that," I said with a grin. "It was several years ago, possibly at Rustermans; I was with Lily Rowan."

"Of course—Lily, now I recall it. A delightful girl. I haven't run into her for a long time. Do you still see her?"

I said I did, and that she had sent her best. All the while, I was getting a very thorough once-over.

"Mr. Goodwin, I love your suit—is it a Ralph Lauren?"

"It's a Bloomingdale's markdown," I said, "but thanks

anyway. Now, Mrs. Forrester-Moore, the reason I'm here—"

"That's such a clumsy name to say, isn't it?" she asked, flashing her pearly whites. "I wish you'd just call me Lucinda, everybody does. I was married once, but I held onto my maiden name, Forrester, too. Perhaps that was silly, but I wanted to keep part of my old self. And I'm sure I know why you're here. It's about Milan." Her expression became instantly sober. "I read that your Nero Wolfe is interested in the case, although I can't imagine why. Don't they think they've caught the murderer?"

"Mr. Wolfe isn't so sure, and because he's a genius, I take his word for things and try to humor him."

"I'd love to meet the man sometime," she said, tucking her feet under her. "But how can I be of help to you now?"

"Well, Mrs. Forrester—Lucinda—you and Mr. Stevens had been together a lot in the last few months, and I thought perhaps you might have some insight as to who might have wanted him dead."

"The police stopped by and asked me the same thing," she said, shrugging and rolling her round blue eyes. "I'll tell you what I told them: If Milan had enemies, I wasn't conscious of it. Mr. Goodwin, he was a very private person, especially about his work. He rarely talked about the orchestra when we were together, and I never brought up the subject. I think one of the reasons he enjoyed being with me was that he could escape from that part of his life completely." She accented the last word.

"I can appreciate that," I said, "but maybe without realizing it at the time, you heard a remark from Mr. Stevens or overheard something said to him that might be significant. Surely he didn't keep everything to himself."

"Oh, no, occasionally he'd bring up the Symphony,

but not often at all." She did the eye-roll again. "The only time I can remember his making a negative comment was about Mr. Remmers."

"Jason Remmers?"

"Yes, although it was just a passing remark, something about how he felt Jason was losing confidence in him. But Milan didn't seem too concerned at the time. I shouldn't have even mentioned it to you, it was so insignificant."

"How long ago was that?"

Another shrug. "Oh, maybe two or three months. Really, it was just an aside, nothing important. I'm sorry I brought it up."

"Did he ever talk about anyone else in the Symphony? Mr. Meyerhoff, perhaps. Or Gerald Milner, or—"

"No, Archie—may I call you Archie? I hate formality. No, honestly, it wasn't like him to speak about the job. He spent so much time on the orchestra as it was that he didn't like to think about it after hours." She shifted in her chair and adjusted her hem to give me a glimpse of a sandaled ankle and a trim calf. "I want as badly as you to see the murderer punished, probably worse. But why doesn't Mr. Wolfe think Gerald Milner did it?"

"Beats me. As I said before, he's a genius, and he doesn't usually share his thought processes with me. I assume you were aware that Gerald Milner and Maria Radovich were serious about each other?"

"Yes, I knew that," she said, looking down and smoothing her gown over her lap. "I had only met him once, in the lounge at Symphony Hall, I think it was. Now that you mention it, Milan *did* bring up his name once or twice, and it was obvious that he wasn't overly fond of him. He seemed like a nice young man, though, and I was shocked about . . . what has happened."

"Can you remember specifically what Stevens said about him?"

"Oh, it was something like 'I don't know how Maria could be interested in him.' Like the Remmers thing, it was just a passing comment, he didn't go on about it. When I said I thought he was nice, Milan changed the subject."

She paused and frowned. "Maybe you already know this, but Maria has never been, well, *friendly* to me. Oh, I understand why. Milan was a father to her, and I suppose she would be naturally hostile to any woman he became attracted to. About Maria—I've tried to call her several times since . . . that night, but there's always no answer. I'd like to do anything I can to help her, if she'll let me. Do you know where she is?"

"I think she's staying with some friends," I said. "If I see her, I'll tell her you've been trying to reach her. You mentioned Milan Stevens being fond of you: Did you plan to get married?"

"You ask direct questions, don't you? I suppose that's understandable in your line of work," she said with a tired smile. "Once was enough for me, Archie. I wouldn't call my marriage perfect, but my husband was a good man, and a generous provider." Her eyes moved around the room as if to underscore the statement. "We had no children, neither of us wanted any, and since I've been a widow, six years now, I find I like the freedom of living alone. I have lots of friends, lots of activities. And besides, Milan never asked me. I'm not sure he fancied the idea of getting married again either."

"If I'm not mistaken, you went out with Charles Meyerhoff at one time, too," I said.

Lucinda laughed. "You know a lot, don't you? Oh, Charles and I went to some parties and plays at one time a few years back, but it was just a thing of convenience for both of us. Nothing serious. I just like to be around people in the arts. I come from a theatrical family myself, Archie. My father was an actor back in Europe, and we lived all over the Continent when I was young. I did a little acting myself for a while, but it was only amateur things. I didn't inherit his talent, I guess. Are you sure I can't mix you a drink?"

"Thanks again, but I'd better be on my way," I said. "I appreciate the time you've taken. One more thing: Can you recall where you were Wednesday night, say, from about seven-thirty to nine?"

Another tired smile. "You have to ask that, of course, Archie. I realize you have your orders. Yes, I can remember what I did Wednesday. I knew Milan would be home working that night—he planned his schedule far in advance, even down to which nights he stayed home working on scores, and he didn't deviate from that schedule. We had been invited to a small late supper up in the Eighties—by some people named Morrison whom I've known for many years. Lawrence Morrison's in the phone directory, on East Eighty-second, if you want to check. I went alone. I think I got there about eight-thirty."

"And before that?" I asked.

"Well, at about seven I realized that I had forgotten to get flowers to take to them, so I left here early, about seven-thirty, I think, and caught a cab in front. We must have tried six or seven florists before I finally found one that stays open late. And I did end up getting a very nice arrangement."

"You wouldn't happen to remember who the florist was, would you?" I asked with a grin that was intended to show that the questions were friendly.

She fluttered a hand. "Oh, it was someplace down on Lexington, I think. Honestly, Archie, I don't remember because I stopped at so many. I'm sorry."

I couldn't see that there was anything else to talk about, so I got up to go and thanked her again. "I do wish I could be more help," she said, standing next to me and looking up with those stunning blue eyes. "While we were sitting, I didn't realize how tall you were."

There was probably a snappy retort to that line, but I couldn't think of it, so I said thanks one last time and eased my way toward the door with Lucinda at my side. She made me promise to keep her posted on developments and we said good-bye—with a handshake. Maybe it's my ego, but I had the feeling she would have preferred a more intimate parting gesture.

On the way down in the elevator and walking along Park Avenue, I tried to analyze her, and then decided I'd dump the whole thing on Wolfe, since he's the one people hire. I ruled against stopping to see Lily, and instead ducked into a drugstore with a pay phone. Jason Remmers answered himself after two rings, and I told him about Wolfe's plan for tomorrow.

"Sunday afternoon, eh?" he said after I'd laid it out. "Well, there isn't a concert, so that's no problem. I'll start calling them right now; I'm sure they're all in town, so that shouldn't give us any trouble. If I ask them to see Wolfe, they'll do it. What time?"

On Sundays, Wolfe doesn't have the usual routine, so I told him four o'clock would be fine, and Remmers said he'd call back later to let me know the outcome. Back outside, the snow had covered the sidewalk and was still falling, but I needed the air to clear away the memories of Lucinda's perfume. The walk would get me home just about the time Wolfe came down from the plant rooms.

## 16

In fact, it was five minutes after six when I walked into the office, and Wolfe was already behind his desk. He scowled and set his book down, knowing that I wouldn't let him get any reading done until I'd reported.

"Number one," I said, "Remmers is arranging to have the trio here tomorrow afternoon. Because you didn't give me a time, I said four. Number two, I've just been to see Lucinda the Hyphen, and her alibi for Wednesday night isn't any better than Remmers's. I assume you want it verbatim?"

Wolfe nodded and rang for beer.

"Okay, but before I start, a few observations about her," I said, "since you trust my instincts when it comes to attractive women. And she *is* an attractive woman, for sure. It's easy to see why Stevens went for her. I'm not ready to give any odds one way or the other on whether she did it, but she didn't seem terribly unhappy. No black veils or anything like that. And she made it clear that she wouldn't mind if we got to know each other better."

"Indeed? Did you find out the extent of her friendship with Mr. Stevens?"

"You said to use intelligence guided by experience, didn't you?" With that, I gave him the whole thing, word for word, although I was interrupted by two phone calls. The first was from Remmers, who reported that he had reached all three men, and they would come tomorrow at four, although he said they weren't very enthusiastic about it, particularly Hirsch and Meyerhoff. About five minutes later, Saul called and said he and Fred were ready to report. I checked with Wolfe, who said they should come after dinner. Between the calls and Wolfe's questions, it took well over an hour, so that when I was through, it was time to go into the dining room.

The shock of being back at work must have worn off, because I was beginning to appreciate Fritz again. His scallops were magnificent that night, and when Wolfe complimented him, his smile wrapped all the way around his face.

Saul and Fred timed it perfectly. We were just finishing our first cup of coffee in the office when the bell rang. I opened the door, helped them off with their coats, and told Saul that Lucinda had proposed to me. After they were settled in the office with coffee of their own, Saul cleared his throat and began.

"The building is fairly typical for the neighborhood," he said. "Nine stories, brick. I talked my way in as a Buildings Department inspector making a periodic check. I've got a card that looks good, and it usually works." I held back a smile and saw that Wolfe was doing the same; the left corner of his mouth was twitching.

"As to access," Saul continued, "there's the front door and the lobby, of course—Archie, you've seen those. In the lobby is one passenger elevator, automatic. Also, they have a service elevator and an interior fire stairway in the rear of the building. Both of them open on a small service lobby on the ground floor. That lobby" —Saul paused for a sip of coffee—"opens out onto a gangway that separates the building from the one next door. The only exit from the gangway is an iron gate seven feet high that fronts on Seventy-sixth Street to the left of the building as you face it. The gate has a panic bar on the inside, so anyone can get out by pushing it, but from the sidewalk, you can't get in without a key. The doorman on duty told me he lets tradesmen in through that gate, but only after checking with tenants to make sure they're expecting someone. He's got a key to the gate attached to his belt by a chain, and when he goes off duty, he turns it over to the doorman or hallman on the next shift."

"Is it possible to go from the gangway through to the next street?" Wolfe asked.

"Not without a ladder or wings. There's a brick wall about ten feet high that separates the property from the building behind it. I'd scratch that possibility. As to staffing, this place isn't as well covered as the big castles over on Park. There *is* a hallman on duty around the clock—that's three of them in all, in eight-hour shifts. The one you mentioned, Tom Hubbard, works four to midnight weekdays. But the building has a doorman only from six in the morning to seven at night—two men each work six-and-a-half-hour shifts. If anyone needs a taxi at any other time, the hallman has to go out and flag it."

"Anything else?" Wolfe asked.

"I'm afraid not," Saul said apologetically. "As it was, I was stretching my inspector's role. With what's happened in that building, the super and everybody else there was jumpy. I had to try to make this seem like a routine check of the exits, the stairways, what-have-you. Luckily, there hadn't been a real inspector around for a while."

"Satisfactory," Wolfe said. Saul Panzer can do no wrong as far as he's concerned, and he knew Saul always feels bad if he doesn't deliver what he thinks is one hundred and ten percent. Now it was Fred's turn, and we all shifted our attention to him.

"Well," he began in his deliberate way, "I followed your instructions, Mr. Wolfe. I didn't try to see Hubbard at all, but I did walk along the block and talk to several doormen. These guys have to all know each other, but the first couple weren't much help. One thought I was a reporter, and he wanted money before he'd tell me anything about Hubbard—I didn't know if there was anything to tell, so I said no thanks. And another one clammed up when I finally admitted to him that I was a private cop. But then something happened that was sort of interesting." Fred stopped, wrinkled his brow, and looked at Wolfe as if asking permission to go on. Wolfe dipped his head a fraction of an inch.

"Actually, it started with a coincidence," Fred said. "A doorman about six doors east of the murder building on the other side of the street is an Irishman—named Callaway. He's a talkative guy, and I struck up a conversation with him, it wasn't hard. Well, it turns out that our people come from the same county in Ireland, and possibly even the same town. Anyway, you're not interested in that, I know, but it's what got us started. Okay, after we'd been chewing for a while out in front of his building, I asked Callaway if this wasn't the block where the big murder happened. He says yes, and I begin asking, just in conversation, you know, about the building and if he knew anybody who worked over there. He tells me he doesn't think a lot of the way the place is run, that it's not well maintained, that it's got poor security, what with a doorman for only part of the time, while his building has one all night. It wasn't hard to shift the conversation to this guy Hubbard, and Callaway says he knows him. What's more, he says he hasn't got much use for him. I asked why, and he said something like 'I don't respect a man who chases after prostitutes, even when he's working.'

"I wanted to know what he meant, of course, and he told me that everybody along the block, all the doormen, knew about how Hubbard had a thing for hookers, particularly redheaded ones. I asked how he knew, and he said that sometimes the girls would hang around the building in the evening, trying to make a score with him."

Wolfe made a face. "Do these women normally infest that neighborhood?"

Fred shifted in his chair. "Not really—at least as far as I know. Their usual territory is farther south, close to the big hotels. But I think a few work their way north sometimes."

Saul sensed Fred's discomfort and cut in. "Yeah, he's right, Mr. Wolfe. The action is in midtown, but some of the streetwalkers do go up farther, particularly if they can get a regular customer. If the word got around about this character, it's possible a few might drift by to see if they could develop some business."

Wolfe scowled again. He had once described prostitution as an unimaginative vocation peopled by unhappy practitioners catering to unpleasant clients. When I asked how he knew, he glared at me and went right on talking. Whether you agree with Wolfe or not, New York has plenty of practitioners, particularly of the streetwalker variety. For anyone who spends much time outside, they seem easier to find than a taxi, and they come in all shapes, sizes, colors, and ages, including some pathetically young ones.

"I was sort of interested in the hooker angle," Fred went on, "so I asked Callaway if by chance there'd been any of them around Stevens's building the night of the murder. That made him a little suspicious; when he asked why I wanted to know, I told him I was a private cop working on another case in the neighborhood, and I said I had just wandered down this block out of curiosity to see the murder site. He seemed to buy that. He said that on Wednesday night there'd been a big party in his building, and he was so busy opening car doors and ushering people in that he didn't notice what was going on down the block. He said the first he knew something had happened was when a police car parked in front of Stevens's building later in the evening. Around eleven o'clock, he thought."

As Fred went on, Wolfe seemed to lose interest. I could always tell; his eyes traveled around the room—to the bookshelves or the clock or the globe. By the time Fred had finished, he'd already rung for beer, and I took orders from the others. Fred had beer also, and when Saul asked for cognac, I decided that sounded good for me, too.

We resettled with our drinks, and Wolfe began asking Fred about the block: the relative position of Callaway's building to the murder site, the width of the street, the size of the trees. He's grasping, I thought, trying to show us he's at work, but he really doesn't know where the hell to go. I was ready to cut in when he stretched both arms out in front of him, palms down on the desk. It's not a gesture he uses often, but the few times I'd seen it before, it preceded an order.

"Saul. Fred. You can say no to this if you want to. Indeed, I won't blame you if you do; were our positions reversed, I would almost certainly refuse the assignment myself, out of both helplessness and distaste." He inhaled and let the air back out slowly. "I want to know if a prostitute, redheaded or otherwise, called on Mr. Hubbard when he was at work Wednesday. And if so, I want her brought here." He leaned back and took a sip of beer.

"Lovin' babe," Saul said just above a whisper. "There must be five thousand of 'em in New York." He took a sip of cognac and turned to look at Fred, who was staring down into his beer glass. Then they looked at each other, and Saul turned to Wolfe. "I think we should get started right away," he said. "I've got a few ideas on how we should proceed, and I'd like to talk them over with Fred." They each took one last swallow and got up to leave. To be hospitable, I walked them to the front door and wished them luck. There was no joking this time, only handshakes.

Wolfe had just poured his second beer and was glowering at the foam when I plunked down at my desk. "Helplessness and distaste, huh? A cute little phrase, but you knew damn well that they wouldn't turn you down, even on an insane go-around like this."

"Archie, I won't argue the merits of the assignment, but I've never known Saul or Fred to be intimidated by what you call long odds, and besides, the thorough hunter can ill afford to overlook any thicket, however dense."

"So now we've gone from fishing to hunting, have we? Okay," I said with a shrug, "you're paying them, and for Saul alone, that's a hundred-and-a-half a day now, plus expenses."

Wolfe returned the shrug and opened a seed catalog. "Are the germination records current?"

That's another of his conversation-ending lines, so I pulled out the records, which were in fact not current, and began working, but only after I'd treated myself to a cognac refill.

## 17

It snowed all morning, so that by noon the plows were whining and scraping outside on Thirty-fifth Street. I'd slept late, and by the time I got myself together and went down to the kitchen, it was ten-fifteen. Wolfe wasn't around; on Sundays, he abandons his weekly schedule, usually staying in his room until at least noon. Fritz was ready for me with a pot of coffee, the Sunday *Times,* and sausage links and wheatcakes ready to go on the griddle. He asked how the case was coming, but I told him to try me later, maybe tomorrow. This was the fourth day since the murder, and already the *Times* had bumped Milan Stevens off the front page. They did have a long page-three story, though; it said that a spokesman in the D.A.'s office hoped that Gerald Milner's trial could begin "in the next few weeks." Further down in the story was a mention that the Stevens memorial service would be held Monday afternoon.

After polishing off six wheatcakes and five sausage

links, I refilled my coffee mug and went to the office. My desk calendar had just the single notation for Sunday: I had penciled in "three from Symph." at four P.M. Turning to the phone, I dialed Jason Remmers's number, and for the second time in as many days, he answered himself. He was only too happy to provide what I asked for: thumbnail biographies of the three who were coming to see us today. I took down his comments in shorthand and thanked him for his trouble, then did my own editing. I typed out brief summaries of each of the three, and by single-spacing was able to fit it all on one sheet, which I put in the center of the blotter on Wolfe's desk. Here's how it read:

CHARLES MEYERHOFF: Age, about fifty. Has been managing director of the Symphony for six years. Home town, Pittsburgh. At one time a violinist with orchestras in Minneapolis and Cincinnati, later had management position with Pittsburgh orchestra before joining Symphony. Known to have quick temper, resented Stevens and his power in the orchestral structure. The two argued frequently. Divorced. No children. Lives alone in the Brompton Arms residence hotel.

DAVID HIRSCH: Age, early forties. Has been associate conductor of New York Symphony for five years. A top-notch violinist, he also is an aspiring composer, but has been unable to get Symphony to play any of his works. Was hostile to Stevens because of this and also because he felt he was passed over for the conductor's job. Austrian by birth, moved to the States in his teens, Remmers thinks. Married, no children, lives in Ridgewood, New Jersey.

DONALD SOMMERS: Age, twenty-eight. Outstanding flutist, has been with Symphony three years, a soloist on numerous occasions. Juilliard graduate and native of Boston, he was a prodigy, played in concert with Boston Symphony as a teenager. Had a deteriorating relationship with Stevens, told Remmers he thought Stevens wanted to drive him out of orchestra. Single, lives on Gramercy Park.

Just as I got back to my desk, the phone rang. It was Lucinda. "Archie, I just remembered something that might be important—you know, on the subject we talked about yesterday."

"Okay, shoot," I said, poising a pencil.

"No, I'd rather not talk about it over the phone. Couldn't you come up?"

I tried to tell her the telephone lines were perfectly safe, but it was obvious she was holding out for another personal visit. I looked out at the snow and shuddered, but said I'd be along as fast as I could. Leaving a note on Wolfe's blotter next to the sheet of biographies, I pulled on overshoes and heavy coat and charged out into the mini-blizzard.

By some miracle I found a taxi within a block and was at Lucinda's ten minutes later; all sane New Yorkers were at home and the streets were deserted. This time I didn't get any of the boredom-and-snobbery routine from the lobby crew. They seemed to be expecting me, and the hallman even gave a fair impersonation of somebody trying to be friendly, which I halfheartedly returned.

Things also went more smoothly inside Lucinda's apartment than the day before. This time I didn't get a twenty-four-minute shuffle. In fact, she was waiting in the white-on-white-on-white sitting room, wearing a gauzy full-length number the color of raspberry sherbet when Miss Mouse ushered me in. "Archie, I'm glad you could come so quickly," she said from a sofa, looking up to be kissed. I aimed discreetly at her cheek, but damned if she didn't turn her face at the last instant and lay one square on my lips, with her own slightly parted.

I had to brace myself or she would have pulled me down on top of her, and for a second I came pretty close to letting her do it. But I finally broke the hold and slid, almost gracefully, onto the sofa next to her. "That was a four-star welcome," I said, smiling and running a hand through my hair. "And as much as I'd like to find out what you do for an encore, I think we'd better get to business. For starters, what was it you remembered that's so important?"

"Oh, Archie," she said, returning the smile and putting an arm across the top of the sofa behind me, "I apologize if I came on so boldly, but I told you yesterday how good-looking I think you are. I guess I just let myself . . ." She trailed it off, and in too studied a way, I thought. "Archie, after you left yesterday, I got to thinking about all the times I had been with Milan, all the things he had ever said that had any connection with the orchestra. There *was* something once, it must have been close to a year ago. It seemed so unimportant at the time . . ." She really liked using the trailing-off trick.

"Tell me about it," I said, lighting a cigarette.

"Well, as I remember it, we were right here in this room, having drinks. By the way, can I get you something?" I shook my head and she went on. "Milan was quite upset that evening. It seemed that he and Mr. Hirsch had a meeting in Milan's office at Symphony Hall to talk over some orchestra matters, routine things. I gather they would meet often to do that. Anyway, this day there was a strong argument—I can't even remember if Milan said what it was about. But Mr. Hirsch started the argument and became very agitated. Milan said that at one point he stood up, banged his fist on Milan's desk, and said something like 'I'd kill before I saw this orchestra go to hell. And if things keep on this way, that's where it will go.' I may have the words a little wrong, Archie, but that's basically what he said.

And he used the word 'kill,' although you know how people talk sometimes."

"And you don't know what the argument was about?" I asked.

"I'm not sure Milan ever said. What I remember most was how upset he got about Mr. Hirsch's temper."

"Was he afraid for his own safety? Did he say anything about that?"

"Oh no, no, he never mentioned it. Milan didn't ever seem to fear for himself. I think his main concern was for the orchestra. And he felt his associate conductor wasn't supportive of him."

"Not from the sound of it," I agreed, drawing on my cigarette. "Tell me, why didn't you tell me about this yesterday?"

Her answer was a coy smile. "You made me nervous, Archie. I guess you could say I wasn't thinking straight . . . all those questions, all the strain after what happened."

She was one hell of an actress, that was for sure. She knew where to make the pauses, which words to accent, how to tilt her head. It was almost like watching one of those British whodunit plays Lily drags me to every so often.

"While I'm here and we're on the subject, do you happen to know Donald Sommers?" I asked.

"From the orchestra?" Lucinda paused and pushed back a stray hair. "I don't really know him, but I've met him a few times."

"Did Stevens ever say anything about him, anything negative?"

"You mean he's another one who is suspected?" she asked, shifting to face me.

"I didn't say that." I grinned. "I was just curious because I've heard his name a few times."

"I think perhaps he and Milan had fought over a solo

once. But he is so young—he *looks* so young. I would think of him as just a boy."

"A boy who's pushing thirty."

She shrugged. "Well, I somehow got the feeling that Milan wasn't fond of him, that maybe he would be happier if he were not a part of the orchestra."

"You seem to be remembering all kinds of things that you couldn't yesterday," I said lightly.

"Oh, Archie, please don't tease me. I really can't recite anything specific that Milan said about Mr. Sommers. It's just an impression I got."

"Okay, one last thing before I go. How would you describe Stevens's relationship with Charles Meyerhoff?"

Another shrug. "Maybe somewhat strained. But to be honest, I don't ever remember Milan talking at all about Charles to me."

"Could that have been because you used to go out with Meyerhoff?"

"That of course is possible," she said. "But I never once got the feeling Milan felt any bitterness toward Charles for any reason, and although I haven't seen Charles that much recently, I never sensed any dislike for Milan on his part. But then"—she stretched out both arms palms up and did another eye-roll—"what do I know?"

"You know a great deal," I said, "but whether I'm hearing all of it is a different matter." When she started to protest, I held up a silencing hand and said I really had to go, but that she'd be hearing from me or Wolfe. We wrapped our arms around each other at the door, and I was the one who finally broke the clinch, or we might still be there.

It was harder getting a cab back, and it was after one when I walked into the office. Wolfe looked up from a book, his face a question mark.

"Lucinda F-M is really something," I said, slipping into my desk chair. "Seems she had a sudden burst of

recollection and had to share it with me." I then gave
him a verbatim report, leaving out only the details of
our opening and closing embraces, which he wouldn't
have appreciated anyway. "Has your opinion of her
changed since yesterday?" he asked after I had finished.

"I think I trust her less than I did. Maybe it's all those
damn theatrical poses she strikes," I said. "Also, she
seems to have a very selective memory. If you're looking for odds on whether she did it, I'm still not ready to
give any, though. Maybe that's because she kisses so
well."

Wolfe grimaced and picked up the sheet with the
thumbnail biographies. "They're all still coming?"

"Yes, sir, at least as far as I know. I talked to Remmers
this morning—that's where I got the biographical stuff.
Do you want to see them all at once, or should I hold
them in the front room and bring them in one at a
time?"

"All at once. The interaction may be instructive to
watch, particularly if Mr. Meyerhoff does indeed have a
quick temper. Has Saul or Fred called?"

I said they hadn't and he nodded, then picked up his
book and submerged himself while I went back to playing
catch-up with the orchid records.

If nothing else could be said for that Sunday-afternoon
visit, at least they arrived promptly: My watch read two
minutes past four when the doorbell rang. Through
the one-way panel, I didn't have any trouble figuring
out which body was attached to which name. Meyerhoff
was standing in front of the others, and he didn't look
happy. He was the shortest of the three, with wavy
brown hair that was retreating up his forehead and
probably would disappear altogether in the next ten
years. The one with horn-rimmed glasses had to be
Hirsch, if for no other reason than age. He was three
or four inches taller than Meyerhoff and had a scraggly
mustache, and his face wasn't filled with sunshine ei-

ther. Sommers was a head taller than Hirsch, and even with his black topcoat on, I could see that he was nearly as thin as the instrument he played. He had shaggy black hair and eyebrows, and his own expression was one of worry rather than anger.

The bell rang for a second time just as I swung the door open. "Good afternoon, gentlemen, please come in," I said in a hearty tone. "Awful day, isn't it?" I got only grunts in reply, and my calling each by name as I helped him off with his coat didn't seem to make an impression. "Where's Wolfe?" Meyerhoff demanded. "I want to get this over with fast."

I led them to the office, still playing the hearty butler role. Before I was finished with the brief introductions, Meyerhoff had attached himself to the red leather chair and thrust his chin at Wolfe as if daring him to challenge the choice of seats.

It didn't get a rise. Wolfe acknowledged each of them with a nod, then slipped the gold strip into his book and put it down deliberately. His eyes settled on Meyerhoff, then went to Hirsch, seated next to him in a yellow chair, and finally to Sommers, who had been left with the yellow chair closest to me.

"We can give you a half-hour, no more," Meyerhoff said loudly, looking at his wrist. "We wouldn't have come at all, except that Jason asked us to. I can't see any reason for this, what with—"

"A moment, please," Wolfe said, holding up a hand. "If you'll indulge me in a preface, Mr. Meyerhoff? Thank you. I assure you my admiration for brevity is at least equal to your own. Before we begin, would anyone care for refreshments? I'm having beer."

Meyerhoff gave a vigorous shake of his head, which seemed to set the mood for the others. They also declined, although more graciously.

"Very well," Wolfe said, touching his buzzer and giving them the once-over again. "As Mr. Remmers told you and as you have no doubt read in the papers, I have been hired to identify the killer of Milan Stevens. Now, I—"

"This is crazy!" Meyerhoff roared. "Everybody knows who killed Milan. The police got the right person, and they got him fast. Why can't we just—"

"We seem to be interrupting each other, Mr. Meyer-hoff," Wolfe snapped. "If you please. You've all taken the trouble to brave execrable weather to get here, and I thank you for it. You moments ago expressed your desire that this meeting be brief. It can only be so if you allow me to continue. You'll all have your turn to speak."

"God, you're every bit as arrogant as I'd heard," Meyerhoff said, crossing his arms. Then he gestured to me. "Is he going to stay in here taking notes?"

"Arrogant?" Wolfe asked, lifting his shoulders a quarter of an inch and dropping them. "Perhaps, although I prefer 'self-possessed.' As to Mr. Goodwin, yes, he is present at all meetings in this room. And his faculties are such that if he did not take notes, he could nonetheless reconstruct verbatim a conversation of several hours' duration. I had no idea anyone would object to his attendance. After all, each of you also is a witness to everything that will be said here." Wolfe focused on Meyerhoff, who scowled but didn't open his mouth.

"Now, if I may go on," Wolfe said, pouring beer, "Mr. Milner has of course been charged with murder. He is known to have been in the Stevens apartment on Wednesday night, and is also known to have had a confrontation backstage with Mr. Stevens recently, a confrontation that centered on Mr. Milner's relation-ship with Maria Radovich. These are well-documented occurrences, and I do not quarrel with them. For my own reasons, however, I believe someone other than Mr. Milner killed Milan Stevens."

"And what might those reasons be?" It was David

Hirsch, his Austrian origins showing in a slight accent. He cleared his throat and fidgeted.

"No, Mr. Hirsch," Wolfe said, "as I stated, they are my own reasons, and I'm not prepared to share them right now."

"This sounds like a fishing expedition to me," Meyerhoff barked. "Your reputation for exorbitant fees is well known in this town. You've got a client who doesn't want to believe the man she loves committed murder—the murder of her own uncle. Enter Nero Wolfe. She turns to you, and you accommodate by calling in anyone who ever had words with Milan. Oh, don't think we don't know why we're all here; we talked about it on the way over. Each of us has at one time or another gone at it with him—and me more than anybody, it's true. But we're not alone; there are others in the orchestra who've fought with him or have some reason to resent him. I'll be glad to supply you with names—then you can spend the next month questioning them, too." Meyerhoff, who'd been leaning forward during his little speech, slouched back into the chair and folded his arms again.

"I appreciate your offer," Wolfe said dryly. "I also appreciate the mention of your various disputes with Mr. Stevens. It saves me the trouble of having to bring it up as the *raison d'être* for this gathering." He paused for a sip of beer. "Mr. Meyerhoff, since you brought up the subject, I'll ask you first: What were the bases of your disagreements with Milan Stevens?"

"I assume you know at least a part of the answer to that question already, from your talks with Jason. But as long as I'm here, I might as well indulge you, to use your own word." He leaned forward again, elbows on the arms of his chair. "I've been managing director of the Philharmonic for a little over six years now. When I joined it, the orchestra was in chaos. The music director at that time was incapable of exercising authority and maintaining discipline—I think that's a fair statement, isn't it, David?"

Hirsch nodded, grim-faced. "Yes, in fact an understatement. 'Chaos' is the word I'd use, too."

Meyerhoff went on. "The Symphony board decided after several years of badgering from a number of us that a change had to be made. It was about then that Jason became chairman, and he was strongly in favor of hiring Milan, who at that time was in London. Milan had a well-known name in music circles, particularly in Europe, but from musicians and other orchestra people I'd heard things about him that I didn't like."

"What things?" Wolfe asked.

"Well, for one, his choice of repertoire. Instead of trying to introduce his audiences to some of the lesser-known composers and some more contemporary music, he invariably took a safe 'popular' tack: a lot of familiar, comfortable works—by all the favorite composers. But you'd rarely see him conduct Berg or Schönberg or Bruckner, or give the premiere of a new work. I felt the Symphony should be more innovative and experimental in its repertoire. You need some of the traditional and the popular, yes, but there should be a balance. Stevens simply was not the man to supply that balance." All the while Meyerhoff spoke, Hirsch nodded at varying speeds.

"Another thing was Milan's personality," Meyerhoff continued. "The Symphony needed discipline, yes, but not despotism. This is an orchestra of great individual talents, Mr. Wolfe. For instance, Don here is the finest flutist in the United States, perhaps the world." Sommers flushed and muttered a denial. "Yes, you are, Don, and I'd say it whether you were sitting here or not. Anyway, the Symphony is loaded with great talent, and it takes a skilled, tactful music director to make these marvelously gifted individuals play well together. You don't do that with an iron hand alone; there must be a subtle mixture of understanding and discipline. I know one shouldn't speak ill of the dead, but the truth is that Milan Stevens simply didn't have the warmth to handle the situation. He could keep order, but he lacked the humanity necessary to coax greatness from his players.

"Time and again I talked to him, urged him to loosen up and be more flexible. But the answer was always the same: 'There is no substitute for firmness, and they must know who is boss.' And whenever I suggested he modify his approach, he became angry."

"Mr. Hirsch, do you concur with this assessment?" Wolfe asked.

Hirsch cleared his throat again. "Yes, yes I do. I was also associate conductor under Milan's predecessor, and when Milan was chosen, I was disappointed. I won't deny that I'd hoped I might be picked as music director myself, but"—he shrugged in acceptance—"that was not to be. I resolved to work with the new director, but almost from the beginning, Milan made it clear to me by his actions that I would have almost nothing to say about how the orchestra was run. I often wondered why he even kept me around, but one day I figured it out. It didn't matter who the associate conductor was; under Milan Stevens, he would have very little responsibility, so he probably felt it might as well be me as anyone."

"I understand you have a composition that you hoped the orchestra would someday play," Wolfe said.

Hirsch passed a hand over his forehead. "Yes, that's so," he said after a pause.

"But it was not played?"

Another pause. "No. Milan apparently felt it was not . . . of sufficient caliber to merit a Symphony premiere." Hirsch compressed his lips.

"Why 'apparently'?" Wolfe asked.

"I say 'apparently' because Milan never came right

out and said the symphony wasn't good. But every time I brought it up, he changed the subject or put it off by saying something like 'Oh, yes, we've got to sit down and talk about this when things ease up, but right now is such a hectic time.' He was always too busy. And yet I know it is a good work—I've shown it to many people in the music world whose opinions I respect, and every one has been enthusiastic, far more than they needed to be just to make me feel good."

"Other than its quality, what reason might Mr. Stevens have for not playing your symphony?"

Hirsch shook his head. "I don't know, unless he just didn't want his assistant to get a share of the spotlight."

"Mr. Hirsch," Wolfe said, "was there an open hostility between you and Mr. Stevens?"

Hirsch fiddled with his glasses and uncrossed his legs. "I wouldn't say so. We did argue sometimes, usually in private, about his treatment of some of the orchestra members."

"You thought he was too much the martinet?"

Hirsch nodded. "Yes, he humiliated some of them during rehearsals, shouting insults, generally demeaning them. I felt it upset the whole orchestra, destroyed morale. Instead of getting them to play better, which I assume was the intent, it had the opposite effect."

"This was a frequent occurrence?"

"Yes, at practically every rehearsal. It was as if he enjoyed being so cruel."

"And you reminded him of it?" Wolfe asked.

"Quite often. But he would just brush me aside. 'They are professionals,' he would say, 'and I expect them to play like professionals, not like members of some community orchestra.'"

Wolfe shifted his weight. "Is it true, Mr. Hirsch, that you once told Mr. Stevens you would kill for the orchestra?"

"What?" Hirsch twitched like he'd just gotten a high-voltage jolt. "Who told you that? I never said such a thing!"

By this time, both Meyerhoff and Sommers were trying to jump in. "Gentlemen!" Wolfe snapped it off. It wasn't loud, but it shut all three of them up. "If you please, at the risk of being repetitious, you'll all be able to leave here sooner without interruptions." He turned back to Hirsch.

"It has been said that you spoke the following, or something very similar, at a meeting in Mr. Stevens's office: 'I'd kill before I saw this orchestra go to hell. And if things keep on this way, that's where it will go.' Well, Mr. Hirsch?" Wolfe's eyes narrowed.

Beads of perspiration were forming on Hirsch's nose bridge, above his glasses. He looked at Meyerhoff and Sommers, then licked his lips. "Mr. Wolfe, I never said that, or anything like it." His voice was tense but low, and he accented each word. "I don't talk that way," he continued, gaining speed. "Ask anyone I know. I wouldn't use a word like 'kill,' or even 'hell.' I can't—"

"That's true," Meyerhoff cut in. "I've never heard David—"

"Enough!" Wolfe spat, silencing Meyerhoff. "Mr. Hirsch, please go on."

"I started to say, I can't imagine who would make up a story like that. It just isn't true. I was angry with Milan quite a few times—many times—but I would never, ever say such a thing." He looked around again, at each one of us, and then down at his lap. I started feeling sorry for the guy.

"Mr. Hirsch," Wolfe continued, "can you imagine why anyone would concoct such a story?"

"No, I don't think I have enemies within the orchestra, other than . . ."

"Yes?"

"Other than Milan," Hirsch said, slumping in his chair.

"You considered Mr. Stevens an enemy?" Wolfe asked.

"No, but I think he considered me one," he said.

Wolfe eyed Hirsch. "Were you planning to resign?"

"I had . . . considered it at one time, but recently Charlie—Mr. Meyerhoff—had said there might be a change in music directors before too long."

Wolfe turned to Meyerhoff. The managing director leaned forward on his elbows again. "That's true. Jason had always been Stevens's big defender, and the board pretty well went along with whatever Jason wanted. I've been telling him for over a year how bad the orchestra's morale is, and recently he seemed to be coming around to my view, although he was giving up very hard."

"I gather that if Milan Stevens were to have been fired, it would have been a major setback for Mr. Remmers," Wolfe said.

"Yes, I think that's a fair statement," Meyerhoff said. "He had made a lot out of our getting Stevens originally, and it hadn't improved things at all—in fact, just the opposite."

"Did Mr. Stevens resent you?" Wolfe asked Meyerhoff.

"I'm sure he did—he resented anybody who tried to tell him what to do in any way at all."

"And did you in turn resent him?"

Meyerhoff shrugged. "I guess you might say I resented what he was doing to the orchestra, his inability to pull it together, his refusal to show them any warmth or understanding."

Wolfe drained his second beer and set down the glass. "Lucinda Forrester-Moore had been a frequent companion of Mr. Stevens's recently. Is it true that you and she once spent a lot of time together?"

Meyerhoff smiled for the first time since he'd set foot in the brownstone. "Oh, we'd gone to a number of plays and parties and dinners together—just a thing of convenience," he said gently. "It was never what you'd term a serious relationship."

Wolfe nodded and shifted his attention. "Mr. Sommers, I hadn't meant to omit you from this discussion. Will you share your feelings on your late music director?"

Sommers uncrossed and recrossed his long legs. "They're pretty much like David's and Mr. Meyerhoff's," he said in a high-pitched voice that seemed somehow to go with his build. "He was certainly anything but a warm man, at least in his dealings within the orchestra. As David said, rehearsals were grim affairs, and he often singled out musicians who he felt weren't doing as well as they should.

"I don't want to come on like I'm paranoid," Sommers said, "but I'm sure Mr. Stevens wanted to be rid of me. I could tell by the way he acted whenever we discussed anything one-on-one, such as a solo I was going to do. He always seemed terribly impatient with me. And then there was that newspaper article . . ."

"Yes?" Wolfe asked.

"A few weeks ago in a Sunday interview, Mr. Stevens said that several soloists were more interested in their own careers than in the good of the orchestra. That article ran just two weeks after one of my solos, and I'm sure he meant me specifically. Again, that sounds paranoid, doesn't it? Well, I *do* think he was out for me."

"*Are* you more interested in your career than in the orchestra as a whole?" Wolfe asked.

"I love the Symphony," Sommers said. "It'd always been my goal to play here, even when I was growing up in Boston. I would never have done anything that ran against the orchestra's best interests, and I always thought of myself as a team player."

"Would you have left the Symphony if you felt Mr. Stevens was holding you back?" Wolfe asked.

Sommers looked at both Meyerhoff and Hirsch before talking. "I haven't told anyone this, but now I suppose it doesn't matter. I'd thought a lot lately about leaving. Chicago was interested and so was Boston, and I had some initial talks with people in both places."

Meyerhoff looked stunned. "Don, why didn't you come in and at least talk to me first?"

"I know, I know, I should have," Sommers squeaked, holding up a hand. "But I had to sort this out myself. I didn't want to leave, but . . ."

"You see?" Meyerhoff said, bounding from his chair and leaning on Wolfe's desk with one arm. "You see now what that man was doing to our orchestra? Here's the finest flutist anywhere, a man who loves the Symphony, and he was being driven away."

"Please sit down, sir," Wolfe said peevishly. "Your point is made, and I prefer having people at eye level." Meyerhoff shook his head and sat down. "Thank God you'll be staying with us now, Don," he said. Sommers nodded and smiled weakly.

"Well, Mr. Sommers, it seems that congratulations are in order," Wolfe said, turning back to the flutist. "You've decided that without Milan Stevens, the New York Symphony is a better place to work, is that true? Is that a fair statement?"

"I didn't say that," Sommers croaked.

"But it seems apparent. Do you deny it?"

Sommers looked down and then back up at Wolfe. "No, but I had nothing to do with his . . . death."

"You'll have a chance to prove that," Wolfe said dryly. "We've already gone well over your half-hour, Mr. Meyerhoff," he continued, looking at the wall clock. "Because this is a murder investigation, two basic questions need of course to be asked of each of you: One, did you kill Milan Stevens, and two, where were you Wednesday evening between seven and nine o'clock? Would you like to start, Mr. Meyerhoff?"

"Of course I didn't kill him—we all know who did, although I would never have guessed Milner had it in him. As to where I was—not that it really matters—I had a lot of desk work to grind through, so after supper I went back to my office in Symphony Hall and worked until, oh, it must have been close to ten."

"Was anyone there with you?"

"No, I was alone. There's a night watchman, but I didn't see him in the lobby when I left. He must have been somewhere else in the building."

Wolfe turned to Hirsch.

"Did I kill Milan? Definitely not," he said curtly. "And on Wednesday night, my wife was out playing bridge. I stayed home reading and listening to music. And to answer your other question, yes, I was alone from about seven until, well, it was ten-thirty or so when she got home. But I can assure you I was there the whole time. We live in New Jersey—Ridgewood—and I took a commuter train that got me there just after six."

Wolfe turned to Sommers, who swallowed hard and uncrossed his legs again. "A classmate from Juilliard was in town from Denver," he said, "and we went to the theater that night. I think I may still have the stub at home if you want to see it."

Wolfe shook his head. "No, that's not necessary, but I'd advise you to keep it. Is your friend still in New York?"

"He's gone back to Denver, but I can give you his name and phone number if you want to—"

"Don, this is ridiculous!" Meyerhoff snapped. "This man isn't a policeman, you don't have to explain anything to him. Let's get going—we've given him too much time already." Meyerhoff was on his feet, and the other two looked uncertainly at Wolfe, who made no move to stop them. They tramped to the front hall, with me at their heels. Meyerhoff already had his coat on, but I was quick enough to help Hirsch and Sommers with theirs. I said good-bye, but only Sommers replied; the others were already on their way out and obviously not in the mood for parting pleasantries.

Wolfe was sitting behind his desk in a pout when I walked back into the office. "Jovial group, eh?" I said. "It looks like all we accomplished was eliminating Sommers, and even that isn't for sure. It's simple enough to find ticket stubs and friends who'll lie for you."

"Bah," Wolfe said, glowering at the clock. He put his hands on the chair arms and made the supreme effort to get himself erect, then headed for the kitchen, undoubtedly to monitor Fritz's progress on dinner.

## 18

My clock radio woke me Monday morning with the news that it was still snowing and that the seven inches that had fallen in the last twenty-four hours were a record for the date. To hell with records. When I went down for breakfast, Fritz started asking about the case again, and I told him that as far as I could see we were nowhere. "But wipe that long look off your face," I said. "At least there still *is* a case."

Fritz went right on looking glum anyway, and for that matter, I was a little on the glum side myself. After the three music men had left yesterday, Saul and Fred both called in, and neither had anything to report. "Archie, I've talked to more streetwalkers today than most traveling salesmen meet in a lifetime," Saul moaned, "and that includes a fair share of redheads. But nothing. Even after I convinced them I wasn't a cop, most of them said they never work that far north. Not enough action. I gotta go now—it's almost dark, and like werewolves, they come out at night, in case you didn't know."

I told him that's what I'd heard and gave him a keep-at-it pep talk that really wasn't necessary. I fed the same pep talk to Fred when he checked in half an hour later, only with him, it was needed. He had two reasons for his dark mood: one, he hadn't had any more luck than Saul, and two, his wife, Fanny, wasn't exactly doing handstands over the assignment. But he signed off by saying he was headed back into the streets. "Intrepid fellow," I said, hanging up.

If Wolfe was disturbed by their lack of success, he didn't show it, preferring to concentrate on the *Times* Sunday crossword. After dinner when we were back in the office with coffee, he finished the puzzle, tossed it aside with disdain as he did every week, and looked at the clock, which read eight-fifty-five. "What time is it in London?" he asked.

"Let's see, they're six—no, make that five hours ahead of us," I answered.

"Far too late to call Mr. Hitchcock," he said. "All right, we'll telephone him tomorrow after lunch." He picked up a book and began reading. I decided not to give him the satisfaction of asking why he wanted Hitchcock. Geoffrey Hitchcock is a private investigator in London whom we've used on a number of cases; we've also been able to help him a few times ourselves, which keeps things pretty well in balance. In fact, just a few months before, Hitchcock had called about an American con man who'd shifted to London and was bilking widows and divorcees. Using the *Gazette* clips and the recollections of one of Lon's best police reporters, I was able to give him a good rundown on the guy's methods, for which he was grateful. And Wolfe got a letter from him a few weeks later saying that in large part because of our help, the con man was in jail and Hitchcock collected a fat fee from an angry victim.

As soon as Wolfe got settled at his desk Monday morning following his plant-room playtime, I swiveled to face him. "Big Ben is at this very moment chiming four o'clock," I said.

He breathed deeply and scowled. "I haven't even seen the mail yet, but I suppose you'll hector me until we make the call. Confound it, yes, go ahead and get him."

Hitchcock's number was on a file card in front of me, and with the grace of New York Telephone, I had no trouble getting through. He answered on the second ring, and I nodded to Wolfe, who picked up his instrument while I stayed on the line.

"Mr. Hitchcock? This is Nero Wolfe. How are you, sir? . . . Yes, I'm in good health also, thank you. When we spoke a few months ago, I said we might ask your help again someday, and that day has come. Yes, it's a case—the murder of Milan Stevens."

Hitchcock said the London papers were filled with stories on it, and he already knew about Milner's being charged. He started asking questions, but Wolfe cut him off. "Mr. Hitchcock, I can't at this time tell you very much because I don't know a great deal myself, although Mr. Goodwin and I are certain that the killer has not yet been found. What I need from you is information on Stevens's activities in Europe before he came to America. He was a conductor in a number of places—London, of course, Milan, Munich, and . . ." He turned to me.

"Vienna," I added, and he repeated it to Hitchcock.

"My question is this: Was there an occurrence in one of these cities that could have resulted in an intense enmity toward him? I'm interested in anything you find, however trivial the incident might seem."

Hitchcock said he could check easily enough in London himself, and that he'd call a colleague in Frankfurt to find out about Stevens's years in the two Germanic cities. "I know a man in Italy who may be able to help there," he added. "I suppose you're in a hurry for this?" Wolfe said yes and Hitchcock promised to get back to us within a day. Having thus indulged me by conducting business—all of two minutes' worth—Wolfe submerged himself in reviewing the mail and filling out the order blanks from two new seed catalogs.

That afternoon, Stevens's memorial service was held at three. I thought about going, but decided I would be of more value at home in case Saul, Fred, or Hitchcock called in while Wolfe was up with the plants. None of them did, though, and about four-thirty the cabin fever was so bad that I told Fritz to cover the phone while I went for a walk. The air was cold and clear, ideal for sorting things out, I said to myself. But as I started east on Thirty-fifth Street, I couldn't find anything to sort. We were noplace, and I began to think maybe Wolfe had spent too long on the shelf, like an outfielder who holds out until May and doesn't get his batting eye back before August. Both the Saul-Fred project and the Hitch-cock thing seemed like the long shots of a gambler who was way behind and trying to catch up fast. I was still muttering when I got back to the brownstone at five-thirty after having walked a good four miles. "Only one call while you were gone," Fritz said as I hung my coat up. "Miss Adjari, a little while ago. I told her Mr. Wolfe was with the plants, and she said not to disturb him, but to tell him that the services for Mr. Stevens were very nice and that she is going back to London on a plane this evening."

"Not wasting any time, is she?" I snapped, and Fritz said something about only being a message-taker. When Wolfe came down at six and settled in behind his desk, I told him about the call. The reaction was a shrug and a request to turn down the thermostat. "A damn good idea!" I said, standing up. "A little less heat might stimulate some mental activity around here—God knows we could use it. Maybe if I open a couple of windows too, we'll—"

"Archie, shut up. You're prattling. What would you have me do? Buy advertising time on television? Or erect a billboard on Times Square? Like good fishermen, we have put out our lines. And also like good fishermen, we need to exercise some patience."

"What do you know about fishing?" I snarled as I turned the heat down. "You haven't dropped a hook in the water since the invention of the reel." There was more to our conversation, but that's enough to give you the flavor, and also an indication of why there wasn't much talking at the dinner table, despite Wolfe's attempts to start a discussion on what New York would be like today if the Dutch hadn't got muscled out by the English a few centuries back. It was also quiet in the office after dinner, and when the phone rang, I almost knocked over my coffee cup reaching for the receiver.

I expected Saul's voice, or possibly Fred's, but it was Hitchcock. "Hallo, I've got a little bit for you," he said as I motioned Wolfe to pick up his instrument. "It's quite late here, you know, but I just got a call back from Frankfurt, and I knew you were anxious. First off, I should tell you that the chap from Italy was no help. Seems Stevens's years there were most uneventful. And I could find nothing here in London, either, except for some general grumblings that he was a strict taskmaster. But as to Munich," he said, "my associate in Frankfurt tells me there was one untoward incident. Happened about fifteen years ago, he can get the exact date if you like. It seems a young oboe player in the Munich orchestra named Wald, Willy Wald, was dismissed by Stevens, and rather summarily, at that. Anyway, the young man was killed in a motorcar crash less than a week later. He was alone in the car, and it went off a cliff in the Bavarian Alps for no apparent reason. The authorities ruled it an accident, but there was speculation in the press at the time about suicide. Rather nasty, as you can imagine.

"Stevens defended himself by saying that Wald hadn't been playing well enough to remain in the orchestra. The business got a good bit of publicity for a few days, but according to my Frankfurt friend, it blew over, and Stevens went on to conduct in Munich for several more seasons. I'm not sure this is of any help to you, but you said you wanted anything beyond the ordinary."

"Quite so," Wolfe said, "and I thank you for robbing from your sleep to report this. Anything else?" Hitchcock said there wasn't, and we signed off.

"Well, is that what you were expecting?" I asked.

"I don't know," Wolfe said, leaning back in his chair and lacing his fingers over his belly. He stayed that way for several minutes, then blinked his eyes and reached for his book. I started to say something, but the phone rang.

This time, it was Fred. "Archie, I've gotta go home now, or all hell will break loose with Fanny. I've had hookers laugh at me and swear at me and try to do business with me, but no luck on what we're looking for. I'm whipped."

I cupped the mouthpiece, telling Wolfe that Fred wanted to pack it in for the night, and he nodded. "Okay, make for home; maybe tomorrow will be better," I said, hanging up. "Who am I kidding?" I told Wolfe. "Tomorrow will be more of the same, and we all know it. Let me go and talk to Hubbard; if there was a hooker around the building that night, I'll find out."

"No," Wolfe said, shaking his head. "We can always do that later, if necessary. Maybe Saul will bring us news."

But Saul didn't. At eleven-twenty, he called in and said he'd talked to more than three dozen entrepreneurs of the street, without success. "But I want to keep at it, Archie. Ask Mr. Wolfe to give us some more time."

"Oh, he will," I said, watching Wolfe coax the last

few drops of beer out of his glass. "In fact, I think he may give you another month if you want it. Well, it's his money—enjoy yourself." Saul hung up, and I told Wolfe the day's excitement had been too much for me, that I was going up to bed. He looked up, nodded, and rang for more beer.

## 19

Tuesday was a Xerox of Monday: snow, although now just flurries; Wolfe at his desk reading and ignoring me; and Saul and Fred somewhere out there searching for a woman who might or might not exist. I clipped my nails, shined three pairs of shoes, changed the ribbon in my typewriter, and took two suits to the cleaners. Maria called just after lunch, and I told her we had several lines out. She was back staying with Lily, although she said she could face the apartment now and might move back tomorrow. I suggested she stay put for a few more days.

"The company does Lily good," I said. "Gives her somebody to spout off to about why the Democrats are God's chosen people." Maria laughed for the first time since I'd met her, and it sounded nice. I told her that if she felt up to it, I'd take her and Lily to Rusterman's that night for a quiet dinner in one of the small rooms upstairs. She said thanks, but Jerry was coming over and they just wanted to be alone and maybe would take a walk. Not to be totally spurned, I got Lily to the phone and made a date for the two of us. Lily Rowan rarely says no to a dinner invitation.

She was oozing questions about our progress, and I told her that I didn't think we were doing so hot. "But I haven't been that candid with Maria," I said, "so please don't make a liar out of me when you talk to her. We haven't got forever on this, although Wolfe's acting like it. The D.A.'s office may move slowly sometimes, but on this one they'll be trying for a fast wrap-up. I guess I would too, in their place."

At a table upstairs in Rusterman's, Lily eyed me over her wineglass. "M'love, are you absolutely convinced that Milner didn't do it?"

"Aren't you?" I asked back, doing my eyebrow trick. "You've had plenty of time to observe him the last few days. Do you think he's a killer?"

She shook her head and smiled. "I really don't, and I like to think that intuition of mine that you talk about so much really works. But who else have you got?"

"You'll have to ask my boss about that. For all I know right now, he thinks it's a suicide, that Stevens had a triple-jointed right arm and stabbed himself in the back."

That was enough business talk for the evening, and Lily knew it, so we drifted into other areas, such as who was divorcing whom in her crowd and why. That was hardly a favorite topic of mine, but Lily was so entertaining that for one stretch of at least six minutes, I didn't think once about the murder. Finally, though, she must have noticed me sneaking peeks at my watch, and for the second time in a week she suggested we should be going. "I know you're busting to be back at your desk, Escamillo. Just promise me that when you bust the case wide open—how I love that phrase—you'll let me be one of the first to know." I promised I would, and then dropped her off at her place in a taxi, arriving home myself at just after ten-thirty.

If I didn't know about Wolfe's obsession with meal schedules, I would have sworn he hadn't moved since I left. He was in the same position with the same book and the tray with two beer bottles and a glass in the same place on the desk. It even seemed like the beer in the glass was at the same level. "Anybody call?" I asked, dropping into my chair. "Saul? Fred? The mayor? The president?"

"Nobody," Wolfe said. "Was your meal good?"

I told him it was adequate, and he nodded. After Marko Vukcic's death, Wolfe had been trustee of Rusterman's for many years and had paid close attention to the cuisine and the operation. He also had made it a practice to dine there regularly, though he would have preferred being at home. Since the end of his role as trustee, he felt—and I agreed—that the quality of the food had dropped off, although for my money it was still the best spot in town for dinner if you didn't count an old brownstone on West Thirty-fifth.

"We had flounder tonight," Wolfe said, keeping his eyes on the book. "It was superb." He was getting back for my needling in the afternoon.

"Happy to hear it," I said. "They call fish brain food, don't they? Any results yet? At the rate we're moving, Milner will be doing life before we decide whether to take Saul and Fred off the job of interviewing *filles de joie*."

Wolfe set his book down and looked at me. "Where did you learn that idiom? I salute your literacy, if not your pronunciation."

"Let me translate for you," I said. "It means—"

"I'm aware of what it means," Wolfe said with a scowl. "As to the translation . . ." The sentence trailed off and he leaned back slowly in his chair, closing his eyes. I started to say something but checked myself. He sat that way without moving for quite a while, about five minutes, while I watched him, waiting.

Then it happened. At first, it was just a twitch, but soon the rhythm started. His lips began pushing out and in, out and in. I stayed still, but even if I'd said something, he wouldn't have heard it. When he's like this, no one and nothing short of a nuclear explosion can reach him. Because I've got a thing for timing, I looked at my watch when it started, then went to the liquor cabinet, poured a brandy, and settled in at my desk.

Forty-three minutes and two brandies later, Wolfe opened his eyes, taking several deep breaths. "Bah, I've been wearing blinders," he announced. "The truth has been screaming like a banshee from the housetops, but I've kept my ears plugged and my mind closed. The road has been littered with signs, and I've ignored them all. Get Saul. Get Fred. Call them off. This has been needlessly prolonged."

Perhaps by now you've figured it out too, but I hadn't. When Lily first read this, she said she realized what had happened about the same time Wolfe did, but I told her—as I have in the past—that when you're in the middle of things, the truth isn't as easy to spot as when you're paging through a manuscript. And besides, by the time Lily read this, she already knew how the story ended.

I asked Wolfe for some answers, and just as I did, the phone rang; it was Saul. "Archie, I've got her," he said. "She's right outside the phone booth and scared silly. Does Mr. Wolfe want to see her?"

"Saul," I told Wolfe, cupping the phone. "Good things seem to be coming in bunches. He says he has the lady you're looking for, and he wants to know if he should bring her over."

Wolfe nodded grimly. "Yes, Saul, come ahead," I told him. "Have you heard from Fred? . . . Well, if you happen to see him, call him in." I hung up and swiveled to Wolfe. "Okay, I think I'm beginning to get a glimmer now. Let me tell you where I am, and you can plug the holes."

For the next twenty minutes, Wolfe did fill some holes, although by then I was starting to add a few things up myself. When the doorbell rang, I went to the hall and could see that she was a redhead, all right, and not very happy. When I swung the door open, Saul introduced her simply as Mindy, and after I took both their coats, they trooped into the office.

Through the years, Wolfe has reluctantly questioned a lot of women, but this was the capper. Mindy was wearing a tight maroon sweater, beige miniskirt, and knee-high white spike-heeled boots, not to mention the long red hair that tumbled down over her shoulders. I put her in the red leather chair, and Saul took one of the yellow chairs.

"I ran into her on Fifth near Sixty-seventh," Saul told Wolfe. "She didn't seem interested in talking about anything except business at first. Then when I asked about whether she ever worked up in the Seventies, she started to walk away, swearing at me. I grabbed her, though, and told her I wasn't with the police, but that I knew a lot of them and might turn her in if she didn't help. Right, Mindy?"

She cursed and turned to me. "What's the bit, anyway? Who's the fat guy? I haven't given anybody a hassle. To hell with this." She rose to go, but Saul put a firm hand on her shoulder, and she sat back down. He looked at Wolfe and went on: "Anyway, I got her to tell me that she was up there Wednesday night. With Hubbard. I said that if she didn't talk to me, it would be worse with the police."

Wolfe considered Mindy. "Madam, I can't guarantee you protection, that's true; but it's safe to say your chances are better if you come forth voluntarily."

"But you're not a cop, right?" Mindy said, uncrossing her legs and sitting up straight in the chair.

"Correct," Wolfe said. "However, you're in a spot. We know who you are, and if we report you to the police, it will be far worse than if you admit you spent a portion of last Wednesday night with Mr. Thomas Hubbard." Wolfe was playing a weak hand; we didn't in fact have her name—none of us had seen any identification yet. But she was jumpy and knew she couldn't get out of the house easily. She licked her lips and looked at me with what she thought must have been an appealing expression, but all she got in return was a noncommittal smile.

She turned back to Wolfe and Saul again; the game was over. I poured a brandy and handed it to her, and she took a sip before Wolfe started in. This time, she opened up. Her name was Mindy Ross, from Pennsylvania, and she was twenty-three. She said she'd been in what she called her "current line of work" for eighteen months, all of it in New York. She answered each of Wolfe's questions about Wednesday night, and her description of what had happened was just as Wolfe had been telling me when Saul called.

If he was feeling smug, Wolfe didn't show it, though he had every right to be. "Archie, Miss Ross will be staying with us tonight. Show her to the South Room and explain our alarm system to her."

"Wait a damn minute," Mindy spat. "Nobody said anything about stayin' overnight. I've got to be out—"

"You don't have to be anywhere," Wolfe snapped. "You will stay at least through tomorrow. And you will probably have to make do with men's pajamas, but if you wish, some fresh clothing can be purchased for you in the morning."

I was standing next to Mindy now. She looked up at me and then at Wolfe and back at me again. She swore softly and stood, letting me direct her up the stairs to the room on the third floor behind mine where Milner had been the most recent guest. "This is the place," I said. "We weren't expecting a guest, but I think you'll find things in order. Mr. Brenner is the closest to you in size in the house, so I'll get a pair of pajamas and a robe from him. I'll also see that you get breakfast in your room, say, at eight-thirty.

"Now, as to what Mr. Wolfe mentioned: When I go to bed, I hit a switch that turns on alarms in this house. One of them is just outside your door, so that if you try to step out into the hall . . ." I gestured with both hands to show the futility of such a move. "And even if you got out of your room, you wouldn't know how to open the front door—it's got a special lock. Any questions?"

She had slumped down on the bed, and was sitting there looking like she was about to cry. The hard façade was gone. "Geez, what's gonna happen? I wasn't lookin' for any trouble. I've had enough problems with the cops, I don't need this." I said something I thought would be comforting, but it didn't help, so I walked out and closed the door behind me.

Back in the office, Saul had poured himself a brandy, and he and Wolfe were talking. "Plotting for tomorrow?" I said, sliding into my chair.

"Yes, I was just telling Saul that I want everyone here tomorrow night at nine, including him and Fred. We'll also need Miss Radovich, Mr. Milner, Mrs. Forrester-Moore, and all those people from the Symphony that we've talked to, including of course Mr. Remmers. And the hallman, Mr. Hubbard. I've asked Saul to bring him here; can you arrange for the rest to be present?"

"All in a day's work." I shrugged. "I suppose you'll want Cramer, too?"

Wolfe nodded. "I'll call him myself and suggest he bring Sergeant Stebbins."

For another half-hour Wolfe sketched the plan for tomorrow. We were interrupted once, by Fred calling in to report. I told him Saul had found our woman, and that he should stop by in the morning for a fill-in on the evening's schedule. "Well, it's been nice working for Mr. Wolfe again," he said, "but Fanny's going to be awfully happy when this one's over."

"Believe me, it's almost over," I said, hanging up and turning back to Wolfe.

## 20

It wasn't hard following through on my assignments Wednesday morning. I started with Jason Remmers and got him at home. "Mr. Wolfe has an important announcement about the Stevens murder," I said into the phone. "He asks if you could be in his office at nine tonight, and he wonders if you could ask Misters Meyerhoff, Hirsch, and Sommers to come again, as well." Actually, Wolfe had asked *me* to get all the orchestra people, but I figured they'd take more from Remmers. He said he could make it that night, and that he'd call me back on the others. "It's extremely important that everyone be there," I stressed before we hung up.

Next was Lucinda. "You told me the other day that you always wanted to meet Nero Wolfe," I said when she answered. "Now's your chance. He thought you might like to be here at a gathering at nine tonight; it's to do with Mr. Stevens's murder."

"Oh, Archie, I already have plans," she said. "Do you

know what he's going to say?" I told her I didn't have the foggiest idea. "Well . . . if you really want me to be there, all right, I'll cancel my engagement. For you, Archie." I said Wolfe and I both appreciated it, and that we'd see her at nine.

Of course Maria gave an emphatic yes when I called her at Lily's. "You've found something out, haven't you?" she asked.

"I can't say for sure, but I do know that Mr. Wolfe wants several people to be present—including Gerald Milner." She promised to bring him along and kept pressing me for more information until I politely ended the call.

At ten, Fred stopped in to get his instructions. He was a little unhappy that Saul had been the one to locate Mindy, but it was more than offset by his relief at being able to quit what he called "the great hooker hunt."

Just after he left, Remmers called back, saying that all three from the Symphony would show up. "They don't like it much though," he said, "especially Charlie and Dave." I told him that was life and said we'd see him at nine.

Wolfe came down from the plant rooms on schedule. He rang for beer, and after a quick shuffle through the mail, asked about my progress. When I said we'd lined up everyone for the evening, he told me to dial Inspector Cramer. "With pleasure," I said, punching out the number from memory and staying on the line.

"Mr. Cramer? Good morning, this is Nero Wolfe. I wanted you to know that several people will be here at nine tonight, at which time I'll be discussing the murder of Milan Stevens. I think you will want to be present as well."

"Goddammit, I've told both you and Goodwin to butt out of this. As far as I'm concerned, the department's finished its job on the case," Cramer said.

"It's your privilege to think that, of course. But I should tell you that whether you're here or not, I plan to proceed. You can read about it in tomorrow's *Gazette*, as Mr. Cohen will undoubtedly be interested in the results."

Cramer spat a word. "Is this going to be one of your asinine charades in front of a big crowd?"

"I wouldn't choose that phrasing, but if you're asking if my office will be crowded, the answer is yes. Despite that, we'll have room for you, and for Sergeant Stebbins as well, if you care to bring him."

"I'll bring whoever I damn well feel like!" he bellowed, hanging up.

"Count on Mr. Cramer being here—with a friend," Wolfe said, leaning back and closing his eyes.

The day crawled by, maybe because I was checking my watch every two minutes or so. At four-ten, Saul called to say he'd found Tom Hubbard at home. "He was just as happy to see me as Mindy had been," Saul said. "I laid out what we knew about last Wednesday, which got him. He told me he had to work tonight, but I said that if he didn't come, the cops would probably show up later in the evening and drag him off anyway. That did it; while I was there, he called somebody to substitute, and I'm picking him up at eight."

I gave Saul a "Satisfactory" and then called Lon to tell him we'd have something late tonight for tomorrow's editions, an exclusive. He wanted it all right then, but I insisted that he'd probably have to wait until at least midnight. He said he'd be in his office all night, if necessary.

After dinner while Wolfe was sitting at his desk with coffee, I began setting up: extra ashtrays, chairs from the front room, a fully stocked bar on the small table in the corner. Fred had come at seven-thirty and was upstairs in the South Room with Mindy Ross, who'd gotten a fresh change of clothes, courtesy of a shopping trip Maria had made in the afternoon.

Saul arrived on schedule at eight-thirty with a jittery Tom Hubbard, who looked like he was going to pass out when he saw me. When he recovered, he tried to ask me what was going to happen, but I just nodded to Saul, who steered him into the front room and closed the door behind them. Now we were ready for company.

At eight-forty-three, the bell rang again. It was Inspector Cramer and Sergeant Purley Stebbins. "Ah, Inspector, you could make it after all," I said as they tramped in. "And you brought a date. It's been a while, Purley." Stebbins, who's worked with Cramer for eons and has had what he considers too many dealings with Wolfe and me in the past, nodded his long bony face but didn't smile. But then, Purley Stebbins isn't noted for his smiles, particularly when I'm around. At that, I guess you could say we've gotten along, more or less, through the years, considering our respective lines of work. He may not be the smartest man in the department, but you'll never hear me knock his courage or his loyalty. If I had to pick one guy to be on my side in a bar brawl against the Pittsburgh Steelers' defensive line, it would be Purley, although I'd never give him the satisfaction of telling him that.

"You're the first," I said, leading them to the office and explaining the seating. "Mr. Wolfe will be in shortly, and so will some others, I hope."

"Hah, he's waiting till they're all here so he can make one of his grand entries," I heard Cramer say to Stebbins as I went back to the hall. And he was right: Wolfe had gone to the kitchen at eight-fifteen, ostensibly to help Fritz with the menu planning for the next week, and said he'd be back in when everyone was seated.

They all arrived within about three minutes: first Maria and Milner, holding hands and trying to look brave; then Meyerhoff, looking just as mad as when he'd come last Sunday; then Hirsch and Sommers together, both tight-lipped and grim. Right behind them came a smiling, pipe-puffing Jason Remmers, and finally, in a white fur stole, Lucinda Forrester-Moore, who reached up and pecked my cheek as I closed the front door. "I'm the last one, aren't I, Archie?" she said with an impish giggle as we went in.

"Last is often best," I whispered, steering her to the chair nearest my desk.

Everyone else had taken the seats I'd directed them to. The front row had Maria in the red leather chair, Milner next to her, then Sommers, and of course Lucinda next to me. In the second row were Remmers, farthest from me, Meyerhoff in the middle, and Hirsch behind Lucinda. There were two more chairs against the wall, but both Cramer and Stebbins chose to stand.

I made such introductions as were necessary, including Cramer and Stebbins, then went behind Wolfe's desk and pressed the buzzer to signal him. Next I asked for drink orders. "What's this with drinks?" Meyerhoff demanded. "I certainly didn't come here to socialize. In fact, I didn't want to come at all; I'm only doing it as a favor to you, Jason," he said, turning to Remmers. "And for the second time, at that. And where the hell is Wolfe, by the way?"

"I was wondering the same thing," Hirsch piped in. "And I agree with you, Charlie. This is ridiculous. Here we are in a room with a man who's been charged with murder, and we're going to listen to another man who isn't even an officer of the law. And yet"—he turned to look at Cramer and Stebbins—"the police themselves show up and seem to tolerate this. It's absurd!"

Remmers cleared his throat. "I want to say thanks to you both, and to you too, Don, for indulging me tonight. And as long as I'm here, I'd like to order, Mr. Goodwin. Scotch on the rocks, please. Am I drinking alone?"

Sommers also had a Scotch, and Lucinda ordered brandy, but the rest passed. Just as I handed out the drinks, Wolfe appeared at the door, surveyed the scene, then strode in, detouring around the crowd to get behind his desk. He bowed slightly before easing into his chair.

"I, like Mr. Remmers, appreciate your coming tonight," he said, eyes moving from right to left and back again. "I've met you all except Mrs. Forrester-Moore. Madam." He dipped his head a quarter of an inch and she nodded, smiling. "I trust you've all been introduced, and that you've met Inspector Cramer and Sergeant Stebbins?"

"Yes, and I want to know why they're here," Meyerhoff rasped. "This gathering wasn't presented to us as official police business."

"And indeed it is not, Mr. Meyerhoff," Wolfe said. "These two gentlemen are here at my invitation and remain at my sufferance." He raised his eyebrows. "I didn't think any of you would object to their presence, though. Or am I incorrect?" His eyes swept the arc of faces again and were met with silence.

"Good, then we'll go on," he said, readjusting his bulk and ringing for beer. "One week ago tonight, as we all know, Milan Stevens was found stabbed to death in his apartment by his niece, Maria Radovich. As you also know, Mr. Goodwin had been waiting downstairs and arrived on the scene just moments later. The reason he and I knew Miss Radovich was that she had feared for the safety of her uncle and approached us for help.

"The source of her anxiety was three threatening letters her uncle had received by mail in the previous two weeks. She brought them to Mr. Goodwin and me, and they now are in the possession of the police. Miss Radovich told us her uncle had thrown these notes away and that she had retrieved them from a wastebasket. Is that correct?" he said, turning to Maria. She nodded and shifted in her chair.

"The first of the notes," Wolfe went on, "was mailed to Mr. Stevens shortly after he and Mr. Milner had quarreled in a corridor backstage at Symphony Hall, an exchange that was witnessed by several people. Not surprisingly, news of the quarrel quickly spread throughout the Symphony structure. The subject of this argument—actually it was more a diatribe by Mr. Stevens— was Maria Radovich, whom Mr. Milner hoped to marry." Milner's face and neck were red, and he kept his eyes aimed at his lap.

"Simplicity itself," Wolfe said. "The incident in the corridor, followed by the notes, and then by Mr. Milner's visit to the Stevens apartment on a night when the uncle, who was violently opposed to the marriage, was known to be home alone.

"And then the body, discovered shortly after Mr. Milner's visit. It would all seem to fit together, which is what the police and the district attorney's office even now believe. In fact, it was so neat and clean that I briefly considered Mr. Milner a suspect myself. Could he not have planned and executed this murder, intentionally having all the evidence focus on him, and then argue that only a fool would so totally incriminate himself? Possibly, but he did not make that argument at any time after the murder. And I was also quick to reject this theory because, with due respect to the officers present, the police department has not been noted for its appreciation of subtlety. One might well commit a crime and purposely make all the signs point to himself in order to be thought innocent—only to have the police arrest him anyway without looking further. And in the murder of one as well-known and esteemed as Mr. Stevens, the law-enforcement establishment would be—and was—especially anxious to make a fast arrest. If there was an obvious suspect, they would quickly seize him to still the public outcry and relieve the pressure from above.

"I was also troubled by the notes. Mr. Milner may indeed possess the cunning and courage to plan and carry out a murder, but the sending of those notes made no sense. What would he gain by such action? No, the notes were intended to make Mr. Stevens suffer additionally before his death because the intensity of the murderer's hatred for him was such that even killing was not sufficient punishment. Mr. Milner's animus toward Mr. Stevens, if indeed it may be called that, was a recent development, brought on by their conflict over Miss Radovich. Were he the murderer, his motive would not be revenge, but simply the removal of the only obstacle to his union with Miss Radovich. And the notes were patently vengeful instruments."

"Look, this is mildly interesting in an academic sort of way, but it really doesn't prove a damn thing," Meyerhoff said. "No court would give the least bit of weight to what you've just told us."

"Perhaps not, sir. This was just by way of telling you why I know Mr. Milner is not the murderer. Now I—"

"Excuse me, but I'd like to ask the inspector what he thinks of your line of reasoning," Hirsch said, twisting to face Cramer.

"I think it's so much bull," Cramer said, "but I'd also like to hear what else Wolfe's got to say, so we can all go home before sunrise. I know him better than any of you, and I can say this: Nobody's going to rush him. He'll have his say—all of it—so if you're smart, you'll keep quiet and listen."

"Thank you, Mr. Cramer," Wolfe said. "I'm an admirer of brevity, but we're dealing with a complex consecution of events, as you'll see. Now, after eliminating Mr. Milner, I looked at the other possibilities: There were a number of persons known either to actively dislike Milan Stevens or to at least have reason for being less than friendly toward him." His eyes traveled over the room again.

"Mr. Remmers, you had placed the full weight of your considerable reputation and integrity behind Mr. Stevens's appointment as the Symphony's music director, and the selection had turned out to be disastrous. It would hardly be surprising if you were to feel betrayed by your appointee. Mr. Meyerhoff, you had resented the new conductor's high-handed methods and also questioned his musical depth. And Mr. Hirsch, you were bitter, perhaps with justification, because you'd wanted the music director's job yourself, and also because your composition was ignored by Stevens. As for you, Mr. Sommers, you felt that the music director was unjustly critical of your performance and was trying to drive you from the orchestra." Sommers nodded but said nothing. "Miss Radovich, you were unhappy because your uncle was violently opposed to your choice of a mate." Maria recoiled like she'd been slapped, and started to say something, but checked herself as Wolfe went on. "Mrs. Forrester-Moore, you were frustrated because you did not receive a proposal of marriage from Mr. Stevens."

"That is simply not true!" Lucinda said, leaning forward and clenching her fists. "I know that's been said around town, but it's cruel and it's wrong. As I told Archie—Mr. Goodwin—when he came to see me, I didn't want to get married again any more than Milan did. I won't deny I was fond of him, but marriage . . . no, not at all. You can believe that or not, as you choose."

Wolfe scowled and shrugged. "In any event," he said, "I evaluated these various grounds for hostility toward Milan Stevens. Each of the affected parties may well have had just cause for at least some degree of anger or bitterness, but is any one of these reasons sufficient to fuel a murder?" He looked around the room again, stopping at each face. "I think not. No, whoever ran that letter opener into Mr. Stevens's back had to be driven by more deep-seated emotions—indeed, by an enmity far more intense than would have been generated because of his relatively innocuous acts of insensitivity and callousness."

"Do you call it innocuous when one person tries to destroy the career of another?" It was Sommers's voice.

"I'll answer one question with another, sir. Would—or did—such an action toward you cause you to commit murder?"

Sommers turned from Wolfe's gaze. "Of course not," he said.

"Now, if I may continue," Wolfe said. "Almost from the beginning, I realized that last Wednesday night's violence probably took root some time ago, perhaps long before Mr. Stevens's arrival in the United States. Had I been less sluggish and more visioned, I would have reached the truth earlier, but . . ." He raised his shoulders an eighth of an inch and dropped them.

"Before you start launching into Stevens's life history, let's get a little more basic," Cramer snapped. "How do you explain Milner and the apartment building? Nobody else went in the front way, and the back door is locked from the outside."

"If I may correct you," Wolfe said, "the hallman *says* he didn't see anyone else go in the front way. And I believe him. However, what if he was away from his post at some point during the evening?"

"Conjecture." Cramer sneered.

"No, sir, not conjecture," Wolfe retorted. "The hallman, Mr. Hubbard, was away from his desk—indeed, outside the building—for a period of perhaps ten or fifteen minutes. It was that absence that made possible the murderer's unseen entry into the building."

Everyone started talking at once, firing questions at

Wolfe and at each other. "Please!" Wolfe said over the hubbub. "If I may go on."

"You'd better back up what you're saying," Cramer said, "or I swear to God that you'll be retired permanently this time."

"I'll be the one to decide when I retire, Mr. Cramer," Wolfe said coldly. "And I'm quite capable of backing up what I say. It would be much simpler, however, without interruptions." He leaned back and closed his eyes until all the chatter had stopped.

"Mr. Thomas Hubbard, the hallman in the building where the murder occurred, has an excessive fondness for . . . women of the streets, particularly redheaded ones. This is well-known along the block where he works—it's even something of a joke among his fellow doormen and hallmen, as one of my agents found out on a visit to the block.

"Milan Stevens's murderer also must have discovered this fact—it wouldn't have been hard to do—and put it to use. A prostitute with red hair was located and was paid well to stroll into the building lobby, engage Mr. Hubbard in conversation, and entice him into a car that had been parked down the block expressly for this purpose. It was while the two of them were in the car and Mr. Hubbard was distracted that the murderer entered the building. This was before Mr. Milner was scheduled to arrive and after the doorman had gone off duty for the night, so the front of the building was unguarded. The murderer took a chance on being seen by some other tenant or visitor in the lobby or the elevator, of course. If someone had indeed happened along, the project could merely have been postponed and restructured in a different format; those determined to kill can always find opportunities. Mr. Stevens would have been puzzled by the arrival of Gerald Milner, but beyond that, the evening would have been uneventful.

"But the plan went as scheduled. No one was encountered in the lobby or elevator. The murderer took the elevator to Stevens's floor and rang the bell. Stevens doubtless thought it strange that there was someone upstairs when the hallman hadn't called from the lobby first, but he opened the door to his killer—after all, it was someone he knew well. That the stab wounds were in the back is additional indication of this."

"Wait a minute," Cramer cut in again. "This thing has more holes than the Mets' infield. How did your hypothetical killer know when to go to the apartment and find Stevens home? And how did he avoid running into Milner?"

"I'll try to fill in the holes, sir, if you'll allow me. Everyone in this room probably knew of Milan Stevens's schedule, at least to a degree. His practice was to spend Wednesday nights at home alone going over the scores for upcoming performances. And it was hardly a secret that Miss Radovich had dance rehearsals every Wednesday night, too. Also, the killer knew precisely when Gerald Milner would arrive, because it was the killer who wrote to him on Stevens's own notepaper, asking that he come to the apartment at eight-fifteen."

"This is ridiculous!" Hirsch said. "If Milan was already dead when Milner got there, who told the hallman to let him come up?"

Wolfe frowned and took a sip of beer. "This will be far simpler without interruptions. The murderer wrote the note—Stevens's notepaper would be easily accessible to anyone in this room—asking that Milner go to his apartment. Then, the prostitute was contracted for, undoubtedly in advance. She lured Hubbard from the building at a prearranged time, probably about seven-forty-five, and the murderer went up unnoticed, was let into the apartment by Stevens, and killed him.

"The murderer didn't leave immediately, but rather stayed in the apartment with the corpse, waiting for

Mr. Milner's arrival. When he got there promptly at eight-fifteen, Mr. Hubbard was back at his station in the lobby: The prostitute had been given specific instructions that he must be returned to his desk by no later than five after eight. Milner asked for Stevens, Hubbard dialed the number, and the murderer picked up the phone, probably mumbling something like 'Have him come up'—just a few words, not enough for Hubbard to be suspicious of the voice.

"The murderer, who knew the building well, then moved quickly, leaving the front door ajar to allow entry for Mr. Milner and his fingerprints. The killer then left by the back door of the apartment, taking the service elevator or the back stairway down, then exiting via the rear door and the gangway that runs alongside the building. There's an iron gate to the street that's locked from the outside, but anyone on the inside can open it merely by pushing the panic bar. So the murderer disappeared into the darkness, and Mr. Milner wandered into the apartment calling Mr. Stevens's name, exactly as had been intended.

"The police have the rest of Mr. Milner's story," Wolfe said, looking at Cramer. "He discovered the body and, realizing he'd be the prime suspect, fled in alarm, leaving the apartment as he found it—except for his fingerprints—and leaving the front door open. His running away was a bonus for the real murderer, who probably thought Milner would call the police when he found the body. That he didn't made things look even worse for him than they would have.

"In any case, Mr. Milner's presence in the apartment had been definitely established. And the murderer further knew that because of the nature of Hubbard's absence from the lobby, he, Hubbard, would never volunteer that he had been gone for a few minutes. Hubbard could be expected to state—as he did—that he was on duty all evening and that Milner was the only person who had asked to see Stevens."

"Fascinating but farfetched," Cramer said. "For one thing, who's the hooker? And what does Hubbard say about all this?"

"Why don't you ask him?" Wolfe said, touching the buzzer under his desk. Everyone turned to the door, which in a few seconds was opened by Saul Panzer. Saul stepped aside and ushered an ashen-faced Tom Hubbard into the office.

"Mr. Hubbard," Wolfe said, "we haven't been introduced. My name is Nero Wolfe, and I think you've met Inspector Cramer." Before either Cramer or Hubbard could speak, Fred Durkin squeezed into the already crowded room with Mindy Ross in tow.

"Everyone is here now," Wolfe said. "Inspector, this is the young woman I was telling you about earlier. Miss Ross, do you recognize this man?" Wolfe nodded toward Hubbard.

"Yeah, that's him," she muttered sullenly, "the one I was telling you about."

"What did you tell me about him? Please repeat it."

"He's the one who . . . the car. Do I have to—"

"This is perverse!" Hirsch shouted. "Must we sit through this? What's it proving?"

"Shut up!" Cramer bellowed. "Let her go on."

"Miss Ross, how did you happen to approach this particular man?" Wolfe asked.

"I got money to go there and talk to him and, you know, take him to a car."

"Is the person who gave you that money in this room?"

"Yeah, him." She pointed at Charles Meyerhoff.

"I'm not going to stay here and take this!" Meyerhoff barked, standing up, but Purley Stebbins laid a beefy hand on his shoulder and pushed him back into his chair.

"This is a disgrace," Meyerhoff yelled, "being accused by a whore! I didn't kill Milan Stevens, and I'm not saying any more."

"Technically, that's true," Wolfe conceded, draining his glass and dabbing his lips with a handkerchief.

"What're you saying?" Cramer put in. "You heard the girl."

Wolfe held up a hand. "As I stated earlier, the truth was crying out to me, but I ignored it. First, the same phrase was used by two people at different times. 'It was just a thing of convenience,' they each said. Strange that both would use precisely the same words, unless of course they had rehearsed what they would say, anticipating questions. And why would there be questions, other than in an investigation?

"But as I said, I refused to read the sign. Then, through the efforts of an associate in Europe, I learned that Mr. Stevens some fifteen years ago had fired a young man from the Munich orchestra when he was its conductor, and a few days later the musician drove his car off a cliff, killing himself.

"The dead man's name was Willy Wald, and I ignored yet another sign until Mr. Goodwin by chance used the word 'translate' in conversation, waking me from my slumber. My German-English dictionary translates 'wald' to 'woodland' or 'forest.' Mr. Wald was the younger brother of Lucinda Forrester-Moore. Correct, madam?"

Lucinda had a trace of a smile on her face as she looked levelly at Wolfe. "I'd always wanted to meet you," she said in a low voice. "I'd heard so much about you."

"Just so. Yesterday afternoon, through friends in the press, I found that you are a German native, having immigrated to the United States in nineteen sixty-four, the year after your brother's death. You moved to New York, and a few years later married Mr. Moore, taking

his name, but also maintaining an English approxima-
tion of your own surname."

"It now appears that was a mistake," she said, still
smiling.

"Perhaps," Wolfe replied with a shrug, "although my
ego wants to believe that I eventually would have found
the answer on the duplicated phrase alone. By the way,
I congratulate you on losing almost all traces of accent
in thirteen years."

"Thank you," she said, dipping her head slightly.

"Also, your asking Mr. Goodwin back a second time
was a tactical error," Wolfe said. "You overplayed your
hand. It seemed obvious from his report of that meeting that you were trying to muddy the waters by focus-
ing suspicion on Mr. Hirsch, and to a lesser degree Mr.
Sommers—perhaps as a contingency in the event that
Mr. Milner found a way to prove his innocence." Wolfe
turned to Meyerhoff. "However, sir, you may be interested to know that she did not attempt to throw any
suspicion upon you, despite an opening Mr. Goodwin
gave her to do so.

"When I confronted Mr. Hirsch with the charge that
he had made implied verbal death threats to Milan
Stevens, his reaction was such that I all but eliminated
him from consideration. Patently, talking in that manner was not his style."

Wolfe turned to Cramer, who had moved behind
Lucinda, while Purley Stebbins remained at Meyerhoff's
right shoulder. "I said that I was convinced Stevens's
murder was the result of a deep-seated and intense
hatred. And such hatred could indeed have been sparked
by the death of a loved one—in this case, a brother.

"Lucinda Forrester left Europe shortly after her brother's death, bitter and resentful toward Milan Stevens
but probably resigned to never having the opportunity
for revenge. Imagine how she must have felt, years
later, when she learned he was moving to the very city

in which she lived. Coincidentally, she as a recent widow had been spending time with another member of the Symphony, Mr. Meyerhoff. However, she shifted her attentions to Mr. Stevens soon after his arrival here. Even then, she probably had begun to lay plans for his murder, although I doubt if she shared those plans with Mr. Meyerhoff at that time, and Mr. Stevens, who likely had never met the sister of Willy Wald in the Munich years, was totally unsuspecting. As for Mr. Meyerhoff, he grew increasingly unhappy over Milan Stevens's dictatorial ways, which steadily increased his power within the orchestra—at Meyerhoff's expense. Further, the managing director had grown deeply attached to Mrs. Forrester-Moore.

"This combination of emotions on the part of Meyerhoff was perfect for her purposes. She had for months, no doubt, been contemplating a way to avenge her brother's death, which she had always felt was directly attributable to Stevens. When the maestro and Milner had their public confrontation and word of it got back to her—possibly from Stevens himself—she had an unexpected opportunity. But as plans took form in her mind, she realized the need for an accomplice, and she approached Meyerhoff. You'll have to ask him whether he initially resisted, but in any event she was able to enlist him and they set to work.

"The notes to Stevens at home were her first step because, as I said earlier, even murder was not sufficient satisfaction for her; she wanted his suffering to be psychological as well. It turned out to be a pivotal decision, because the notes were what in effect brought Mr. Goodwin and me into the case—a case that at the time was not yet a capital one.

"Next, the pair set about studying the security in the building where Stevens lived. This was Mr. Meyerhoff's assignment, and he no doubt soon discovered that the doorman went off duty at seven in the evening, which meant that only one person, the hallman, stood between them and undetected entry. Next, Meyerhoff began inquiring about the habits of the hallman, Mr. Hubbard here. He may well have talked to the same person that Mr. Durkin did to find out that Mr. Hubbard had a certain weakness, one that would be skillfully exploited, as we have seen." Wolfe leaned back, took a monumental breath, and poured his second bottle of beer as Hubbard stood near the door, looking at the floor and fidgeting.

"It also fell to Mr. Meyerhoff to locate a woman, which he did, specifying a time when she was to call on Mr. Hubbard—a time after the doorman went off duty but safely in advance of Gerald Milner's arrival. To assure that this part of the operation went smoothly, Meyerhoff accompanied Miss Ross to the door of the apartment building and also supplied the automobile in which she and Mr. Hubbard had their *appointment*. He probably watched them from a place of concealment, making sure that Hubbard was well occupied while Mrs. Forrester-Moore entered the building.

"After she got inside, the rest was simple. She was familiar with the place, having been there many times to visit Stevens. She took the elevator up and rang the bell, and Stevens, on learning who it was, opened the door. They went back to the library, where he'd been working, and at some point when his back was turned, the former Miss Wald, doubtless wearing gloves, plunged the letter opener into his back. The first stab was enough to stagger him, and it was then easy for her, despite her size, to run the blade in a few more times to finish the job. Miss Radovich said she thought the letter opener was her uncle's, so it's possible Mrs. Forrester-Moore took it on an earlier visit to the apartment, with just such a use in mind. Anyway, after killing Stevens, she stayed in the apartment and waited for the call from the lobby announcing Milner. When it came, she probably muttered those few words I mentioned earlier, or a similar phrase. It would have been simple for her, a sometime actress, to approximate Stevens's voice for just a short sentence. After talking to the hallman on the speaker, she had ample time to flee via the back way while Milner was going up in the elevator."

Cramer started to say something to Lucinda, but she spoke first: "Mr. Wolfe, I've very stupidly underrated you. I really—"

"Lucinda, you don't have to talk to him!" Meyerhoff shouted. "He's just fishing. We don't have to stay here and subject ourselves to this slander!"

"Charles, it's done," she said. "Over. Mr. Wolfe, I started to say that despite your reputation, I didn't really think I was in jeopardy, particularly since you didn't even take the trouble to see me yourself until tonight; you sent Archie instead. Not that I minded, you understand." She turned to me with a sad smile, and for just an instant I wished Wolfe had made a mistake. "The only thing you were wrong about was my never having met Milan in Munich. I did meet him once—at my brother's funeral, but he didn't recognize me when we became acquainted here years later; my appearance had changed a good deal." Her hand went reflexively to her hair. "I was glad he didn't remember me, though, because almost from the beginning, I had made up my mind, as you said, to . . . take revenge. I'm not sorry I did it, either. But I am sorry about Mr. Milner. And I'm sorry about you, too, Charles," she said, turning to Meyerhoff, "although your dislike for Milan had grown to be almost as great as mine, I think."

Lucinda shifted to Maria Radovich. "You despise me, as you should. All I can tell you is your uncle had a side you probably never saw: He could be cold, cruel, hateful. He was that way to my brother—and to other members of the Munich orchestra, too. He killed Willy as surely as if he'd been steering the car. He humiliated him in front of the entire orchestra, called him names, derided him. You can see how he treated someone you cared for very much," she said, nodding toward Milner. She sank back into her chair and looked at Wolfe.

"Madam, since you mentioned Mr. Goodwin, I should point out that his eyes and ears are every bit the equal of my own, and in some situations, considerably better. Also, I must tell you that your little speech rings hollow, particularly your solicitude toward Miss Radovich. I, too, know that the man you call Milan Stevens had a dark side, and may indeed have been capable of driving another person to his death. Let us even assume he was the direct cause of your brother's fatal crash."

Wolfe turned a hand over. "So, powered by revenge, you plotted and carried out his murder. Should that not have been enough for you? Indeed, an argument could be made for this act of retribution in the minds of many self-respecting citizens, if not in the eyes of the law. But you had to go further, conspiring to frame an innocent person. The easy assumption would be that you did this to avoid prosecution. I think not; rather, it was your hatred for Mr. Stevens, which was so overriding that you also sought to savage the life of the person he held dearest, his niece, by destroying the man she loved. And the irony is that this man"—he gestured toward Milner—"is of virtually the same station and age as your brother was at the time of his death. Madam, hatred has become your handmaiden." Wolfe scowled and turned to Cramer.

"In case you're wondering, Inspector, you'll find that neither Mr. Meyerhoff nor Mrs. Forrester-Moore has a strong alibi for last Wednesday night. He said he was working late in his office in Symphony Hall, but claimed the guard didn't see him when he left. And she was at a dinner party that evening, or at least told Mr. Goodwin she was. But at the time of the murder, she was supposedly in a cab trying to find an open florist shop. However, I suppose you'll be checking all these things thoroughly."

Cramer glowered at Wolfe, but didn't say anything. There really wasn't a hell of a lot he could say. After all, for the last two hours he and Purley Stebbins had watched their work being done for them.

## 21

After breakfast Thursday, I walked to a news-
stand on Eighth Avenue and picked up the early edi-
tion of the *Gazette*. The banner read SURPRISE IN STEVENS
CASE, and there was a column of type of the previous
night's events in the brownstone, plus pictures of Wolfe
and me. I made a mental note to thank Lon for using
the newer mug shots that I'd sent him.

It had been well after midnight when things settled
down at home and I finally got around to calling him.
He'd griped about the hour, but he had his exclusive,
and the timing was perfect for the *Gazette*, an evening
paper. Now the A.M.'s would be scrambling to catch up,
but they were dead until their first editions for Friday
hit the streets late Thursday night.

I got back to the house and laid the paper on Wolfe's
desk blotter along with his mail just as the elevator
came down from the plant rooms. "Good morning,
Archie, nice to see the sun today, isn't it?" he said,
positioning himself in his custom-made chair. I let him

go through the mail and have a look at the paper before I turned to face him.

"By the time we got everybody out of here last night and I got through filling in Lon on the phone, it was too damn late to ask any questions, but I've got a few," I said.

"Oh?" Wolfe raised his eyebrows.

"Yeah. For instance, why weren't you suspicious about Alexandra Adjari? You didn't seem concerned when she went back to London right in the middle of this mess, but how did you know she hadn't come to New York earlier than she had said? She could have been here for several days before she came to see us, which would have made her a suspect."

"That point occurred to me as well, and one morning I called Mr. Cohen from the plant rooms. Through his connections with the customs people, he determined that Miss Adjari did indeed arrive in New York on the day she came to see us."

"Sneaking around behind my back again," I said. "Speaking of Lon, I suppose he's the 'contacts in the press' that you mentioned last night when you talked about Lucinda's past?"

"Yes, another call to Mr. Cohen when you were out. Through the *Gazette* files and European correspondents, he confirmed what I suspected: that Lucinda Forrester-Moore was indeed a German émigré, and that her name had been Wald."

"But you didn't know that Willy was her brother?"

"No, I couldn't establish that fact definitely, but it seemed almost a certainty. I felt confident in confronting her with it."

I grinned. "There were several things about last night that I liked, but the one that tickled me most was the expression on Cramer's face when he realized there were two of them in on it. I also noticed that you overcame your bashfulness about drinking a certain brand of beer in the presence of the heir. Which leads me to my last question: What would you have done if Remmers had been the murderer?"

The corners of Wolfe's mouth went up slightly, deepening the folds in his cheeks. For him, that's a smile. "I knew you would ask eventually, Archie. It's a measure of your thoroughness." He opened his center desk drawer, reached in, and pulled out four bottle caps, which he spread on his blotter.

I picked one up, then another. "When?" I asked.

"Fritz went out for them the afternoon you were at the bank getting Mr. Milner's bail money."

"Did any measure up?"

"Passable, all of them, and far superior to that unspeakable 'Billy Beer' you saw fit to present to me last summer. I'm pleased that Mr. Remmers was not one of the guilty. Any change would have been a step toward mediocrity, and as Isaac D'Israeli wrote, 'It is a wretched taste to be gratified with mediocrity.' I fervently hope my taste will never become so wretched as to be satisfied with one of these."

With that, he dumped the bottle caps into his wastebasket and rang for beer.

## 22

The phone was out of control all that morning, with newspapers wanting quotes and TV stations begging to bring cameras and crews into the brownstone. I fielded them all, giving the papers a crumb here and there but leaving the electronics guys out in the cold. The most interesting call came just after Wolfe had come down from the plant rooms.

"Archie, we're putting together the second-day stuff on the Stevens case, along with a sidebar piece on you and Wolfe," Lon Cohen said. "And yeah, yeah, we'll use those updated photos of both of you again. But what I want is a quote on whether Wolfe is getting back into the detecting business again."

"That's one you'll have to ask him yourself," I said. Cupping the mouthpiece, I spun to face Wolfe. "It's Lon; he has a question for you, one I can't answer."

He pursed his lips, nodded, and picked up the receiver, while I stayed on the line. "Good morning, Mr. Cohen. What can I do for you?"

"Good morning, sir. First off, congratulations on the case. And we really appreciate the exclusive."

"Thank you. You were a help to us as well, and as I've said, I like to keep our mutual-assistance relationship in balance."

"Yes, well, I hope what I'm going to ask won't throw it off too much. The *Gazette* would like to know—for attribution—if you're going back into active practice again."

"I'm not sure how you would define active practice," Wolfe said. "I've always viewed investigative work as an integral part of my existence. And at the present time I have no plans to terminate my existence."

There was silence on Lon's end. "I take it this means you're returning to work?" he finally said.

"Mr. Cohen, I see no need to elaborate. Again, I thank you for your recent aid. I must leave for another appointment now. Good day, sir."

Wolfe and I cradled our receivers in unison and I looked at him with what was probably a smirk, but said nothing.

"I seem to remember that you're somewhat behind on the germination records, Archie," he said. "I would hope that by day's end they will be current."

I could have given him any one of several answers, but I chose instead to go to the kitchen for a glass of milk. Besides, I was about to break out laughing, and I didn't want to do it in front of the big ham.

## 23

It all tied up nicely. As you undoubtedly know unless you were in Fiji at the time, Meyerhoff and Lucinda got life terms in a short, unspectacular trial. What you may not know if you don't live in New York or read the *Times* is that Maria Radovich and Gerald Milner were married about a month later in a chapel at St. Patrick's. Both Wolfe and I got invitations, and I went. Maria looked stunning, and Milner had tears in his eyes. David Hirsch served a few months as interim music director of the Symphony until a replacement was found, and his composition finally had its premiere, getting what the gossip columnists would call "generally favorable reviews." Last I heard, he was living someplace in New England and I guess doing well with his composing, although I don't keep up with that kind of thing. Both Milner and Sommers are still with the Symphony. The day after Wolfe broke the case, Remmers met with each of them and told them the Symphony valued their talents and wanted them to stay.

We heard this from Remmers when he stopped by to thank Wolfe again. He also tried one more time to write a check as a further expression of his gratitude. I was all for it, but Wolfe said no. "Mr. Remmers, I appreciate the gesture, but as I told you before, I was in effect paying a debt incurred many years ago. I am only now free of that debt." Remmers persisted, however, and Wolfe finally came up with a solution that allowed him to leave the brownstone smiling.

Wolfe did a bit of smiling himself a few days later. A small peach-colored envelope came addressed in a sweeping script to "Nero Wolfe, Esq." and plastered with stamps that had the Queen's profile on them. I open Wolfe's mail as a matter of practice, but I knew this was one piece he'd want to slit himself, so I left it intact on his blotter with the rest of the day's delivery. I was at my desk typing when he opened the envelope, read the letter, and read it again. He finally set it down gingerly and formed his lips in a circle. I kept typing, but I could hear the air passing in and out of his mouth. It's his version of whistling, something I had heard him do maybe five times through the years.

Fortunately, I was spared most of this performance because the front doorbell rang, and Fritz was out shopping. The guy at the door was a burly character who introduced himself as Lou. He needed a shave and had a tooth missing where it showed, but I welcomed him warmly. I told him to take his delivery down the outside front stairs to the basement, and that I'd let him in that door. After all, it was the first of fifty-two weekly calls he'd be making, and I wanted to make him feel welcome. It's not easy pushing a hand truck with four cases of Remmers on it.

S.